The Unforeseen

The Unforeseen

Christian Oster

a novel

translated by

ADRIANA HUNTER

OTHER PRESS • NEW YORK

Copyright Editions de Minuit, 2005, *L'imprevu*
Translation copyright © 2006 Adriana Hunter

Production Editor: Robert D. Hack
Text design: Natalya Balnova
This book was set in A Caslon Regular by Alpha Graphics of Pittsfield,
New Hampshire.

10 9 8 7 6 5 4 3 2 1

Library of Congress Cataloging-in-Publication Data

Oster, Christian.
  [Imprévu. English]
  The unforeseen / by Christian Oster ; translated by Adriana Hunter.
    p. cm.
  ISBN-13: 978-1-59051-265-4
  ISBN-10: 1-59051-265-0
  I. Hunter, Adriana. II. Title.
  PQ2675.S698I5713 2007
  843'.914—dc22

                                                      2006033004

The Unforeseen

Women only have to come in contact with me to fall ill. They catch colds, they sneeze, sometimes their throats are affected. . . . For them, it is the first time. Their healthy days were before my time.

It is my fault: I always have a cold, they inevitably catch it. Once they have recovered, they always leave me . . . and I am left with my own cold.

It gives me something to do: I can go through quite a bad phase then, go down with a hyper-cold, and increase my hankie consumption. When this happens I go out just as much as usual, but not for so long. I feel better lying down, with a box of Kleenex within reach. A heavy cold is good for drowning sorrow: it dilutes it.

Laure was with me when she sneezed for the first time in her life. She was surprised, then distraught. Not me. I am never surprised by other people's sneezing: it is like an echo of my own. In fact I am inclined, when someone near me sneezes, to take out a handkerchief.

I was not surprised, no. But I was touched. I had always found Laure a little distant, and her sneeze brought her closer to me. I felt a sort of acquiescence on her part. As if she were saying she understood me now, she accepted me, and the least she could do, from that day onward, was to come along with me. To come along with me properly.

Because she never really came along with me: she followed me. She found my love disturbing—even before she caught her cold.

She loved me in her own way, a perplexed, restrained sort of way. But, deep down, it was not so much her own love she was holding back as mine. The things I did made her uncomfortable and the things I said worried her. Calm down, I would say, it's just that I love you. That's not very reassuring, she would say.

So Laure started sneezing regularly, but not excessively. Even her cough, which came next, was just sporadic, and not the chesty or tickly sort either, so it could not be ascribed a specific medication. Personally, I gave up finding cures for myself a long time ago and, given her inconsistent symptoms, I advised Laure not to do anything either. It'll pass. To be honest, that is not what I wanted. I liked hearing her sneeze. Hearing her, actually, rather than seeing her. There was always that little delay, a second, no more, when she coughed or sneezed beside me rather than facing me, and I would not be aware that it was her. Someone's coughing, I would think, someone very close to me, but who isn't me. Strange sensation, just for that one second, and before it was over I would tell myself that not only was it not me, but it was in fact her. Laure. And I found that touching.

And worrying too: Laure did not find it touching at all, sneezing irritated her. The first time it happened, with Agnès, I just looked on the bright side. Then, not long after she recovered, she was very quick to split up with me. As if, insofar as those first manifestations could be interpreted as a kind of emotional crystallization, Agnès's cold, viewed through its entire evolution, corresponded to the duration of our relationship.

Luckily, things did not always go that way with other women: there were the ones with colds who I decided to leave, the ones without colds who abandoned me to my fate. . . . There were no rules.

Even so, at the stage when Laure was still coughing—no fever, mind you, she was perfectly mobile—Philippe, whom she had introduced me to when we first met and who could, I suppose, have been my friend but who was originally hers, invited us to spend a few days in Braz.

He wanted to have a party for his birthday, his fiftieth. Given that it was not my own birthday, it was no big deal to me. I can never get excited about other people getting older but there you are, there is always that distance between them and me. No one can stop my getting old like a hypocrite. I keep no count of the passing years: I just carry on, looking forward. The only thing that could put me off is death but until further notice, it is not here, it is somewhere else, busy culling other people. I only know it by reputation and I am pretty sure that when we do meet, things will not go well. No chance of sweet-talking it. So I have no intention of speeding up the process.

When Philippe invited us, then, Laure was coughing, but not too much, and sneezing too, but no more than the coughing. In fact, she was making do with my provision of hankies. One pouch of compact Kleenexes, which hardly took up any room in the suitcase. Two or three packets distributed among my pockets, so that I could hand them to her if and when. Apart from that we took summer clothes because it was nearly summer, and a few sweaters because Philippe was celebrating his fiftieth birthday on an island. An island in Brittany that was likely to be cool and windy in the morning and evening.

We had a good car and I was driving. I did not want Laure at the wheel in the state she was in. Anyway, there was not too much further to go. We were already halfway there, just before Laval. I was holding her hand in mine on my thigh.

So there we were, going away together for the third time in a year. I had moved in with her right away, all she had to do was move her clothes hangers along a bit. A little surprised, she had asked whether I loved her. She was still here.

It was warm, it was a good open road, I toyed with the idea that I was at the wheel of my own life. The scenery changed gradually, a fresher green occasionally appearing from a line of trees. Little corners of paradise surprised us as we carved through them, briefly nostalgic for their virginity. Here and there a cow stubbornly chewing the grass. A stream suggested rather than seen.

Laure sneezed hard. It was her lack of experience, and a need to express herself, which stopped her restraining it. It almost made me swerve. Pulling sharply away from my thigh, her fingers tugged at the packet she had taken from my shirt pocket with the other hand, and, in a twisting movement slightly hampered by the seat belt, took a Kleenex that she did not so much bring up to her face as come to meet, leaning her head forward in a clumsy attempt to reduce the distance. She buried herself in the paper, freed herself from it again, and—rather more calmly—reached for help from a second Kleenex.

"You're really coming down with this cold," I told her.

"Yup," she said.

She was in a bad mood. Once again, I reminded myself that she had no previous experience. My own permanently afflicted nose was like a guild to me, a slight handicap I had learned to deal with over the years. Laure, on the other hand, was squaring up to it, striking out. I wanted to take her hand again, she pulled it away. I had it long enough to ascertain that she was hot.

"I think you're feverish."

"So do I."

Despite the novelty of the theme, it was not the best conversation we had had. I tried to resuscitate it by suggesting we bought a thermometer when we came off the freeway. We wanted to stop at a hotel, anyway, we liked spending nights in hotels. She would have to go and lie down right away.

"Oh no," she said.

"For the night," I told her. "You're going to have to."

She said nothing in reply. She resented me. She had always resented me for loving her, then for loving me. I had never resented her for resenting me. I worked away for the two of us, a bit lonely sometimes. So what, I told myself, if you're better at it than her.

I let go of her hand, which I had taken again. Apart from the fever I could no longer feel her, not one nerve in her fingers. Laure was withdrawing farther than ever. I have to say, her brutality hurt me. You see, my problem is I cannot get used to that sort of thing.

In any event, I could not go on driving like that, with the unresolved question of her fever and its attendant psychological problems still between us. Laure was irritated, I was stressed.

I looked for an exit. I could no longer utter a word. I decided to wait until we had found some common ground before trying to touch Laure again. I concentrated on driving, which meant I completely lost my concentration. It was becoming dangerous staying on the freeway. The only word we shared during that phase, and I am not even sure of that because Laure hardly emerged from her self-absorption, was the one I read on a road sign for an exit: Commency. I took it.

You see, Laure had dark hair.

I loved her eyes.

I was afraid I would lose her.

First I was looking for a drugstore. I found one in Chavrière, five kilometers after we came off the freeway. It was seven in the evening, the place was open. As far as I could tell from the outside, there was no one in the shop. Nearby there were people waiting to buy fresh bread. A young woman went past on roller skates.

I got out of the car. There were two pharmacists, a man and a woman. Both standing behind the counter. I felt as if they were expecting me. The man, slightly older, in his white overalls, was the same generation as myself, but that was where our similarities ended. I do not like white and I could never have been a pharmacist. But the pharmacist, this pharmacist at least, could not have been me. He looked like a specialist. The woman could have been his daughter, ultimately she could also have been a dancer, or an English teacher, or absolutely anything, with her blond highlights. Wild ones, I mean. Much more open-minded. But they both took an interest in me, each as much as the other. It seemed to me as if they had seen me coming for some time.

I asked them for a thermometer and some aspirin. Regular commodities, granted, but they were on the counter right away, apparently without their having to look for them. Even though I was absorbed with other preoccupations, in some inferior sub-strata of doubts I imagined them having the things ready, in preparation for my visit. I am not saying I believed what I thought, but I thought it.

I hardly thanked them. I lingered a while, looking at the metal drawers behind them. I liked watching them being used: one, I pull it open, two, I turn to the side, I read the labels, crouching to have the drawer at eye level, a long narrow drawer with low sides, so that the boxes inside can be seen, and so I find . . . or perhaps I don't, I would have to ask for it. Well, anyway, I would have preferred them to have opened them, those drawers, in their professional capacity, even though I was prepared to concede that I had not asked for anything that required concealing, or isolating, or going to any lengths to find for me. What I mean is that it all seemed too easy, too natural, too expected. It is almost as if I did not really need to open my mouth, me the customer, to explain what I wanted, and now I even wondered whether I had expressed myself properly, before they served me at least. I certainly had formulated my request, yes, but at what stage I do not remember.

I went out, burdened with my ridiculously light carrier bag, with the unpleasant sensation at the end of my arm that I was not actually carrying anything, even though my fingers were gripped around the handles. Proof that I had not gained anything substantial, and yet some change had taken place.

Laure was not waiting for me. Well, she was resting her head, tilting it sharply against the headrest. I sat back down at the steering wheel, slipped the bag into the side pocket, set off and drove around slowly, looking for a hotel and, miraculously—it is always a miracle in that sort of village, but not in this one, the actual one we were in, no, it was not a miracle, just the absence of a disaster—I found one.

A good one, even. Only two stars, but with a garden. With chairs and tables. And flowers. A little porch with steps up to it. The place was actually on the outskirts of the village, set back from the road, indicated by a little sign that I would not have missed for anything in the world. I cut the engine.

"You must have some aspirin right away."

She might just as well have been dead. I realized she was sleeping, but did not savor this triumph. I went into the hotel and asked whether they had any rooms.

"For how many nights?" I was asked as if anyone could envisage a prolonged stay, here in Chavrière, long enough to exhaust some curiosity aroused in the traveler's mind by a brief drive through this village, potentially rich in things to be discovered.

"One," I replied. "We have to leave tomorrow," I added, in consideration of the hotelier who had a welcoming kind of beard, a full one I would say, and I even wondered for a moment whether it had grown since he last had a customer, an incarnation of his long wait. And I glanced anxiously at the walls, looking for signs of peeling paint or any other indicators of ill-used time, a state of abandon that my host would have been the first to have suffered, stuck there behind his desk with only the silent and depressing growth of his beard hair. But no, it was clean, like the exterior, and the deer on the walls stood out clearly from their off-white background, impeccably reiterating their graceful leaps as they escaped the huntsmen.

"I see," he said. I did not know what it was he saw, but he had several rooms available.

"All of them?" I asked, as if ironically raising the possibility of his eventual bankruptcy. I felt like forcing a laugh, and he smiled, affording a wide breach in his beard, as if he knew how I felt because he felt it himself, but without the immediacy, with a philosophical insight, not really as I felt it, and I did not—on this occasion—ask him how he managed to survive here. I just looked at him.

"You have the choice," he told me. And he laid out a series of keys on the counter.

I immediately had a sense of disproportion. Just one woman, I thought to myself, (and not one who was easy to move, either) and all these rooms, that's far too much, and anyway, this isn't right at all, I thought, there's too warm a welcome in this part of the world, everyone's too helpful, but no one's actually helping me properly. I'm alone with her, that's just it, and I wonder whether I wouldn't prefer a hostile environment, really hostile, where I would have to fight for what I want. Oh well, I think to myself.

"I'll only take one," I say to the man. "One key," I explain. "Just tell me which is the best room."

"Number 25, overlooking the courtyard, it's nice and quiet."

I was sure it would be. I wondered where the staff were and immediately had an answer to this question because someone came across the lobby, a short woman wearing homely clothes. The bearded man's wife, I decided, as she shot a glance at me, slightly suspiciously but perfectly legitimately, I felt, given that any non-local presence here required justification, except for philosophers, of course, and—in front of the wife—I asked the man whether, as well as the key, he might be able to give me a glass of water right away because my wife, my one (although I did not need to endorse that fact), was still out in the car, not well, feverish.

"Wait a moment," he said.

He left the counter and reappeared with a glass of water, which I took from him. I went out onto the porch. Laure seemed to be asleep, her head still tilted back. I went over to the car and opened her door.

I shook her gently, this woman who was so extraordinarily asleep, this woman I had been sharing my life with for a year. I did not, on that particular evening as I leaned through the open door, take the time to look at how her face had been rearranged by sleep, beneath the fascinating secret of her eyelids. I was thinking about her aspirin tablet, I had just popped the soluble pill into the glass, probably too soon, because it had already stopped dancing about and was disintegrating, reduced almost to nothing in the closing phases of its effervescence.

Laure still did not wake up. I had to jolt her, thinking to myself that I could have waited for the aspirin, and dissolved another one, once we were in the room, most likely using water from the basin rather than the mini-bar that threatened not to exist at all here, but actually no, I wanted to get her fever down, soon, and to take her temperature before the pill had any effect. Which meant that I was confronted with two emergencies.

"Laure," I said, shaking her by the shoulder, "please, Laure," and she eventually opened one eye.

It was when she opened the second that I realized she was red in the face. I felt her forehead, which was hot, and I put the glass into her hand with some authority. She started to drink.

"All of it," I said encouragingly. She finished the glass, I felt better. But I still had to get her out of the car, to let her know that I had found a hotel and to steer her up to the room.

"Hankie," she said.

I took the packet from my pocket, the packet *I* had not actually used much recently, I realized, less than ten times that day—much less, I told myself now that I come to think about it, but do I really have time to think about it—and handed it to her. I even suggested she should keep it. It was the first time I had made her that sort of offer. She accepted. She now seemed to be yielding to her condition, molding herself into the temporary identity we are perfectly at liberty to adopt when taken ill and that—to a greater or lesser extent—puts us on familiar terms with our precarious condition, even though Laure was one of that large majority of people for whom good health is not only close to being the norm but also a way of life, perhaps even a sort of definition of their character. Laure was in fact giving in by agreeing to keep that packet of tissues, changing her own opinion of herself, even if only in a limited capacity, but—contrary to what I might have expected —I did not find this change reassuring.

"You have to get out of this car," I told her.

I gave her help and encouragement. At the same time I also noticed that the bearded man's wife had come out, displaying a degree of curiosity, which may have been tempered—although I did not take the time to check— by a predisposition to concern. I was concentrating on Laure who, sneezing and wiping her nose on the tissues, was now finding the strength to drag herself from her sleep, perhaps even discovering, when all was said and done, that in the upright position she might be able to evolve to some other state, a temporary recovery of her strength or a brutal relapse. To be honest, I did not have to do much: she went ahead of me, making her way over to the hotel. At this point the woman stepped down from the porch, sidling off toward a lean-to on the outside of the building. I went in behind Laure, empty glass in hand, with the other hand positioned gently in the small of her back to steady her, and we walked past the manager, whom Laure granted an economical greeting while he, conspicuously preoccupied with other things, stroked his beard with two fingers.

I put the glass down on the counter on our way past. We took the elevator and, at a bend in the corridor, we found room 25. I opened the door, nudged Laure inside, closed the door behind us and gauged the bedding with a quick glance.

"Right, I'll go and get the bags," I said. "You lie down." And I went out without waiting for any reply.

As I closed the trunk of the car, I realized I was hungry and that, with good reason, we had not tackled the question of supper. I was worried that this hunger might take a hold and complicate relations, for example if I were forced to leave Laure, who was unlikely to be very motivated on this subject, to go and eat in the village. The hotel did not have a restaurant, at least not as far as I could see.

I went back upstairs and put the bags down in the middle of the room. Laure was sitting on the bed. Just sitting there with her head directly beneath a lithograph of a church, perhaps the one in the village, staring determinedly into space, one hand clutching the packet of tissues.

I asked her whether she had taken her temperature, but before she even replied I knew she had not. She did not reply, anyway. I did insist on that point, making it clear, in a sentence that I fashioned very carefully, having purged it of the excess adverbs that paradoxically suggested themselves because of the urgency, that that very sentence was based entirely on my concern.

"I want you to leave me," Laure replied. "I don't want you to see me in this state. And stop worrying, please."

I did not entirely agree. It was fine by me, this state of hers. Laure being ill, that suited me. I had always helped her when the need arose, always. Rarely, though—that was just it. I was missing out on something. She was making me miss out on something. I wanted to be concerned. To worry, yes. About her. And even, I might as well say it, I had been dreaming of it for the last year, dreaming of worrying about her. Now, here was an opportunity. Except that, to be honest, I was the one I was worrying about. That's not right, I told myself.

I also told myself that, as it happened, a doctor might have done the job better. And so, respecting her wishes, I immediately suggested this scenario as a substitute. I was very happy to be replaced, temporarily, by a doctor. I wanted that, even.

Not her.

"There's no point," she said. "I've got plenty of aspirin. I'll see how I feel tomorrow. But I really want you to leave me."

"Please," she added.

I felt torn. Even if there was one who could be contacted, calling a doctor against her wishes was perhaps not the correct solution, given that Laure had a pretty strong chance of surviving her fever of only a few hours' standing. On the other hand, leaving her, as she was asking me to, put me in a position that I found difficult to envisage. I could, of course, leave the room, but I was preoccupied with the question of coming back. Of the right moment to come back.

"I don't imagine you're hungry," I said.

"No."

"Can't I bring something back for you, at least?"

"No."

Now, if I was not going to bring anything back for her, returning empty-handed, then the question of my coming back at all certainly did arise, my coming back naked, without anything; in short, my coming back, and it worried me going out like that, without a proper motive to come back, and all the while Laure kept staring into space, a space in which I was at pains not to appear, keeping to the side of the bed. She was staring, then, in a way that only allowed for that space and, I gradually understood, was waiting for me to leave so that she could lie down at last, delivered of the weight exerted by the fact that I was simply there.

I resigned myself to this.

"All right," I said. "See you later."

That *see you later* lacked heroism, but, after all, I thought to myself, I can't see why I shouldn't be allowed a bit of slack. I exist, too. Even if, with my cold, I only exist in an average sort of way, for my part. So?

So I left.

I contrived a first staging post for myself: the reception desk. The man with the beard was not at his desk so I waited, drumming my fingers on the counter. It was eight o'clock and I wanted to know whether, in the absence of a meal, I could hope for the odd sandwich. I discovered that I could not when he walked across the hall as his wife had done earlier. Despite my partial loss of sense of smell, I detected a waft of curry from somewhere to the left. Or the right.

"The nearest restaurant is a long way away," he told me. "But you might be able to find something in the village. There's a grocery store that stays open late in the second street after the church."

I went out to the car quickly. In the village, which—when you approach it from this direction—pops up right away as soon as you pass the sign, so that its name seems stuck to it, right onto the village itself, like a label on a model, I could still see some movement: a woman, a dog, a horse trailer pulling in by a pavement. The baker was closed, ditto the butcher next door, and the hairdresser's, and it was hard to imagine—or, at least, I found it hard— that any customers had ever rushed to go there, or gone there at all. What I mean is that, in an unfocused sort of way, I felt worried.

So I took the second left after the church with a good dose of hope, less because I was driven by hunger than out of a need to find somewhere that was open, lit up, inhabited, with shelving inside, somewhere that might indicate a social structure, a sign of life around a solid core. This was in fact the case even though in the early stages I had to navigate around revolving display stands, which were overfilled in places and peculiarly empty in others, without seeing a living soul, be it a customer or a checker. Under the circumstances, I hesitated to serve myself but I did let myself stop and think, standing alone in the glare of the lights from—and the silence disturbed only by the motor of—a refrigerated cabinet, in front of the cheeses, a limited range of them that gave way to the yogurts all too soon and offered themselves rather dispiritingly in the chilled goods section, beneath films so perfectly transparent they revealed textures deprived of contrast and colors devoid of nuance.

I eventually settled on a vague Emmenthal, picked up a loaf of sliced bread a little farther along and, back at the till, noticed an apple nearby. I was soon relieved of it by a helpful hand that transferred it to a weighing scale while a bright voice wished me a good evening, and these two things combined in a clattering of till keys with other elements—printed T-shirt, swarthy skin, thin face—to compose a perfectly soothing human presence that welcomed me like any other local, I thought, without noticing my urban origins.

"Thank you very much," I said.

"Goodnight," the man replied, and I found myself back at the wheel of the car, alone with my doubts.

Obviously I headed back to the hotel. I had been away for forty-five minutes and expected to find Laure asleep, exhausted by the fever. I was not too keen to come back to her awake, ill and ill-disposed toward me.

The man with the beard was reading behind his counter. Seeing my mini-market bag, he gave me a reassured look that was actually equally reassuring, possibly implying that, if there were anything else I needed, he was there with his wife and his reserves. Still, I noted that he had not asked me to eat with them.

I went back up to room 25 and put the key carefully into the lock. The room was silent, and it stayed like that until I padded softly up to the bed; after that even, when I leaned over Laure who had fulfilled my hopes and gone to sleep in the same position I had left her in, with her head poked slightly forward now, her breathing weak and irregular. I took the decision to settle her more comfortably, supporting her lower back with one hand while I held her head with the other in a slow translatory movement toward the foot of the bed. I managed it, at the expense of considerable fear that I might wake her, and that was probably not the only fear that gripped me. I was beginning to feel obscurely afraid in general but, I told myself, we are allowed to feel afraid from time to time, after all, it won't kill us, and if we didn't we would never do anything and, anyway, I love her. And I covered her with a blanket I found in the wardrobe, making sure the top did not touch her neck. Then I watched her sleep.

I felt nervous. She did look serene, granted, but my being there had nothing to do with her serenity that night and could, perhaps, even have threatened to obstruct it. Still, she was asleep and I was there, whether she wanted it or not, watching over her sleeping. And, who knows, perhaps deep down, possibly with the help of the cold and against all expectations, I was keeping her asleep. Neither she nor I could know.

Laure was still just as beautiful, incidentally, just as mysterious and calm, her eyelids so expressive, as if they had their own presence, as if her eyes were closed without truly withdrawing her gaze. The sides of her nose were slightly reddened by her cold that evening, and it was her love that I was looking at, as I had done on those other nights, her love for me watched over by mine for her, with a growing impression that it—her love—was asleep, but that it carried on while she slept without ever going out, of course. In an optimistic way, I was actually afraid it might wake in a bad mood this evening, this love of hers, and I thought that, when all was said and done, I would rather it went on sleeping, yes, even if it weakened a little, just so long as it kept going. And, as Laure still did not wake up, I moved away from the bed quietly and set about using my provisions.

I spotted a chair, pushed right in under a narrow table beneath the window, and I pulled it out and took it over to the foot of the bed, like in a hospital. I sat down on it and put the mini-market bag on my lap. It was still broad daylight, which was normal for June, and through the window, beyond the courtyard, I could see a bit of countryside, the tirelessly blue sky casting its light over us, Laure and myself, in this new configuration that featured the interesting but worrying notion of a bedside vigil. I rummaged through my bag that rustled and was joined by the song of a random bird through the open window, creating a useful background noise for a few seconds. Obviously I did not want to make any noise so it was with infinite care that I took first the piece of Emmenthal, then the pack of sliced bread from the bag.

I did not have a knife. I had not thought of it. My nails, which are quite hard, attempted to pierce the plastic wrapping on the cheese. They slipped. I thought the key to the room could take over from them. I picked it up off the little table, but it clinked against the tag with the number on it. Luckily it clinked quietly, deprived of true resonance between my thumb and forefinger. Laure slept on, with tiny variations in her breathing, which kept me company in my work.

I prodded the key into the Emmenthal, pulled it across and tore both the plastic and the cheese. Piercing the wrapper for the bread posed fewer problems, even though I had to contend with another bout of rustling, of a different kind, which fortuitously coincided with a mowing machine starting up not far away.

At last I could eat something while I pondered the question of my going to bed. In fact, it would be quite simple: I would slip silently into bed beside her and, God willing, we would sleep together. By morning things would have changed. Perhaps the fever would have dropped. Just a warning.

I ate all the Emmenthal with some of the bread, and while I was at it I had the apple, which luckily was not packaged. I bit into it. It turned out to be good and juicy but more than anything else it was crisp, and my teeth, which had just carelessly inscribed their mark on it—suddenly affording me the surprise and the pleasure of overcoming its compact texture, actually buried within it for a moment and stopping the juice from seeping out—had also drawn from it a sharp, almost strident noise. Laure woke with a start, heaved herself onto her elbows and stared at me. I wondered where she had found the strength to open her eyes so wide and, still on the brink of sleep, to hurl such a furious expression at me.

"What are you doing here?" she said, as if I had just committed some terrible crime. "Are you eating?"

I did not attempt to deny this aspect of my behavior. With one final effort, I finished isolating the piece of apple that my teeth had just marked out. I chewed and swallowed. Then I answered yes and looked at her. Given the way she seemed to be defining the situation, I was going to have difficulty avoiding a confrontation. But more importantly, because of her attitude—and perhaps also because of mine—I was struck by a variety of emotions . . . and what emerged was a combination of guilt and astonishment, each of which kept taking the upper hand over the other. And I felt as if I recognized Laure but, at the same time, was discovering her, so much so that I tried there and then to reconstruct a coherent image of her, one that could account for the change that had operated within her.

The fever might have dropped slightly under the effects of the aspirin, because it had been replaced by a suppressed anger that was now gathering momentum as Laure threw me the same cold stare, cold and yet a bit red-eyed too, a sign that she might not actually be any better. Either way, she did not want to say anymore about it, she simply reminded me that she did not want to see me or, more precisely, she did not want me there in front of her.

"Lying down," I said, "I wouldn't be able to see you."

I realized that this was a plea. Things were not going well at all. I waited for her reaction and, as it was a long time coming, I tried to remember us before this episode. Not one image came back to me. Places, perhaps, but not a single scene, situation, or gesture. And yet I had lived with this woman, and I searched for her everywhere in a past that was being erased from my memory by the face she was presenting me with now: embarrassed, hostile . . . more hostile than embarrassed—incomprehensible. In those few moments my love was reduced to a simple knowledge, and I fought against her in the name of that knowledge, scouring her eyes for the love I could not find in them, perhaps it was simply hidden behind them. As usual, I thought. If I dug down a bit, maybe?

Mind you, her face looked as if someone had been doing some digging there, so hollow. It would show itself eventually, I told myself, beneath the fire in her cheeks and the cold fire in her expression, which was all about the fever and her denial of this fever, and her denial of me who was making her ill, confronting me. And her words will come back too, I told myself, the precious words from before, even from earlier today, when she loves me, when she can tell that I love her and she lets me love her, and lets herself love. Well then, you must love her, I told myself, love her better than she does, harder than she does even.

"Listen," I said.

"You could ask for another room," she interrupted very calmly.

I took it badly. I pointed out that she was taking this too far. I reminded her that, incidentally, my love for her implicated me, required my presence. Contact with me even. That it was a small constraint to which I would prefer her to submit. At the same time I avoided mentioning the petty question of my pride: I was unwilling to go to reception and ask for another room.

Unless I just say no to her, after all, I thought. And lie down next to her. Yes, but.

It's more to do with what sort of night we would have under those circumstances, I reasoned with myself.

"You're putting me in an awkward situation," I told her. "Don't you love me anymore?"

No, no, I told myself. You're the one who has to love her. You know that. Not doubt her. Idiot. You forgot for a minute.

So what? I retorted. You're allowed to forget from time to time, aren't you?

What bothers me even more is how she's going to answer. And I know it. That's not the question. It's exactly how she's going to answer.

"Yes," she told me.

Good, I thought.

Except she still looked as if she resented me.

"Okay," I said. "I'm really sorry about this cold. But I didn't exactly inoculate you with it with a syringe."

"That's not the point," she said.

Aha, I thought. I was pretty sure that sooner or later something wouldn't be the point. Which proves that there was a point.

"Another room," she said again. "It must be possible."

She was calming down now, her voice slowing, ready to go back to sleep.

No. She was asleep.

Even sleep can be violent sometimes. I did not know that this woman could be that violent. She had never dismissed me by sleeping before. That's new, I thought.

I looked at her. She's not going to be comfortable sitting like that, I told myself. I'll have to find the energy to move her.

I found that little bit of energy. Then the strength— except it was not strength, it was a decision—to leave the room.

The hotelier was there, behind his counter. He was reading.

"Aren't you in bed?" I said.

"No," he replied. "It's only ten o'clock. Is everything all right?"

"Great," I said.

I had brought my sponge bag. I put it down on the counter.

"I'm going to need a room."

He smiled at me amiably, waiting for a moment.

"You do have other rooms," I said.

"Yes," he said. "Would you prefer any particular one?"

"No. On the same floor, perhaps."

"Number 29?"

"Perfect."

He put the key on the counter. I picked it up.

"Have you eaten?" he asked me.

"Yes," I said. "Thank you."

"Right," he said. "Is that going to be okay?"

"Yes," I said. "Goodnight."

"Goodnight."

He immersed himself in his book again. I headed for the elevator. I really would have liked to know what he was reading. I had forgotten to take my own book when I left Laure. But I did not want to read myself. I wanted to know what the hotelier was reading, that bearded man, with his chubby wife. And the others, too. All the others, at that precise moment, in every hotel in the world. If they were not reading, perhaps they were asleep. Perhaps some of them were doing exactly the same as me. I thought of all the people taking a second room. There could have been several hundred of us in the world, at the time. We constituted more than a group. A population, statistically speaking. We were just dispersed, that was all. Unconnected, with no means of contacting each other. Alone. It was not even worth thinking about.

I arrived at room 29: it was smaller than 25. A man's room, I thought stupidly. For men like us, I corrected myself. Funny, they've given us flowery wallpaper. The bathrooms aren't bad at all. You can see yourself more clearly in the mirror than at home.

I pulled the bedcovers back. Night was settling, but I was not yet. I was just getting ready. I did not know what for. For everything, for exaggeration, excess . . . nonsense. The mysteries of the next day. The best thing to do would be to sleep, I told myself.

I lay down and looked at room 29, lit up by the lamp on the right side of the bed, the side I sleep on. It was dark outside and I had not drawn the curtains. Daylight does not stop me sleeping. I sleep well, anyway. Besides, we don't have to sleep every night, I told myself. Some nights it might be better not to sleep. People talk a lot of nonsense about lack of sleep.

Still, I did think about the journey the following day. I pictured us in the car, Laure and myself. Laure feeling much better, but still there, glad that the fever had dropped and that I was there, me, beside her, the danger over. Everything back to normal. My tissues back in my pocket. Residual sneezing. Chestier cough, but that was just it. On the mend. You couldn't even call it getting better because this wasn't an illness, a cold isn't an illness, it's an inconvenience, it's nothing. It was nothing, I would tell her, you see.

She would nod her head. Her hand would reach for mine.

I closed my eyes. Something different happened.

I saw it all again, absolutely all of it. The meeting, first. The glances, the first words, first gestures, first times.

The first time we walked together.

The first time we had dinner together.

The first time we said good-bye.

We had counted them, the first times. At the beginning. Afterward it became more complicated. We got it wrong. We did not always agree. I also remembered our first disagreement. On the first day. She did not want to see me again right away.

I was tired now. I did not open my eyes again. I had seen all there was to see of my room.

Morning arrived more quickly than I anticipated. Well, I had not really anticipated it. The light was there. So it was the next day, very early. Insofar as I did not remember it but was waking up, I must have slept for a few hours. I felt good. Anyway, I am never depressed in the morning. Allowing for exceptions.

I got up. It was too early for breakfast, I would not get any coffee if I went downstairs. I might as well have a shower and get dressed, I told myself. Which I did, under a firm jet of lukewarm water, my head already feeling cleaned from the inside. No signs of the day before. Me in this bathroom, yes, then back in the room again, getting dressed, alone. A woman, too—all right, she was my woman—sleeping on the same floor. Good, I thought. Good, good.

So, I was living with her at the time. This woman on the same floor. I loved her. She did too. We had set off together, the day before, to meet up with a friend who was celebrating his birthday. His fiftieth. Philippe. Another three hundred kilometers.

A woman I needed to go and see, to find out how she was, didn't I? Oh yes. Who had sent me away the night before. Hmm. I hadn't slept all that badly. I wasn't really that worried about her fever anymore. I don't really believe in fevers, in the morning.

I had the sort of beginnings of an urge to sing something. A tune that I remembered, not an especially melodious one, it did not last long. I went downstairs. The hotel foyer was quite silent. Only the very first birds could be heard through a half open window. The first birds and nothing else, actually yes, a lorry, or a plane, I do not know, it had gone. I went out onto the porch, I could make out the dew on the flowers. It was already warm. The sky was still white, with a red sun between the trees. I set off on the narrow path that led from the porch, skirted around the car park, and snaked across a lawn to the road. A secondary road with a cracked surface and a distinctive camber, and only a hundred meters further on there were already fields and, slightly higher up, some woods. No cars. Behind me, the hotel. Room 25. I did not need to turn around. I knew that Laure was in there, although I did not know in what state. As well as the hotelier. Who may have finished his book, I thought.

In the end I did turn around. I looked at the hotel. I could have lived there. With her, I mean. A hotel with a porch and gravel at the front, I noted. As well as the lawn. And the metal tables. And the small-pane windows. Flowers, but not too many.

I went into the hotel. Still too early for breakfast. I stayed by the reception desk for a bit, looking at the walls, the view out to the courtyard behind, through a glazed door that marked the far end of the corridor with its curtains and tie-backs. I could see an expanse of roof to the left, the top of a stack of wood, a row of lime trees. There was an armchair in the foyer, at the bottom of the stairs. I sat down in it, unable to think. Almost no longer wanting coffee. Needing nothing. I listened to the sounds. The only thing lacking was my book. I would have liked it next to me, closed.

I must have fallen asleep. The chubby little woman was there, not so little, in fact, or so chubby, quite pretty, her mouth, for example.

"Coffee?" she said.

"You bet!" I said, getting up.

I went into a small room with red round-backed chairs, pink paper tablecloths, and white ramekins filled with little parallelepipeds of butter. I was not alone, there was a man, hard to describe him, this man, an early riser, yes, there was that at least; alone, that too, before I arrived, but still alone after my arrival, without a wife, I mean, but not like me of course, *here* without a wife, in his case, well, so I assumed. In the meantime he was indeed alone, facing me, and did not seem to be asking himself the same questions about me, a man who was sufficient in himself, perhaps, quite different from me, I imagined, and he did actually glance up at me briefly before leaning over his coffee cup again. Right, I thought, and I went and plucked a croissant from a basket, and poured myself a glass of orange juice. Then the coffee came, brought by the hotelier's wife. I finished my breakfast, the man was buttering another piece of bread, it irritated me slightly to be finishing before him, what the hell is he up to, I asked myself, he can't be on vacation, this man, not here, what's he waiting for? Why doesn't he get up? Well, I know I've got nothing to wait for, nothing else now, and I got up and, I have to say, I didn't like him very much, that man, nope, I felt no shred of sympathy for him, I didn't even want to ask him about his personal tragedy, because he was going through one, of course.

So I went up to see Laure, I just had to, I had to go up to see her, everyone has their own things to get on with.

The room was silent. I went over toward the bed where, under the sheets, I could clearly make out the contours of a body that, in all logic, must have been hers.

The sheets were moving. Laure's body, then. Shaking from head to foot. I had never seen Laure shake before. But it was definitely her. She was not asleep, just trying to get to sleep. Curled up as if hoping to contain herself. I touched her shoulder.

Her shoulder was hot. She did not react, did not reject me. I called her name gently. She went on shaking and I realized something, although there was nothing I could do about it: I've never made anyone's teeth chatter before.

I went back down to reception. I found the hotelier and not his wife, which was better. I asked him how to get hold of a doctor.

"Is something wrong?"

"My wife's ill. Her teeth are chattering."

He gave me an odd look. How on earth, I read in it, did you leave your wife alone all night in that condition?

Unspoken questions, thanks a lot. I gave no reply. And the hotelier did not press the point. He looked at a piece of paper, dialed a number and handed me the receiver.

I got some secretary, a voice that sounded prerecorded with a standard text, which did not seem to adapt to the situation. I clarified it for her—the situation, I mean—explaining that my wife could not be moved. When you're shaking like that . . .

"Like what?" she said.

I had to describe it.

"Her teeth too," I said.

"I'll put you through to the doctor," she said.

I got through to him, the doctor. He would come, he did not usually do this: basically, I was pretty lucky.

"But you'd better allow an hour," he said.

I thanked the hotelier and went back up to the room. Laure was still shaking.

"I'm cold," she said, still curled up and turned toward the window. I went to the wardrobe to look for blankets. I found two, which I folded in half and laid over the ones already on the bed. Then I lay down next to her, against her back, under the covers.

"There's a doctor coming," I whispered.

My right arm lay along her body, slightly squashed under my own body, my left arm was wrapped as best it could around Laure, joining forces with the obstacle created by her legs that she had drawn up to her, failing to hug her or even to touch some part of her where the bones did not protrude. She was still shaking, and her teeth—when they stopped chattering—clenched together, just as I clutched her, thinking I would prove myself stronger than the fever, warmer than it, that I would manage to overcome the cold that had her in its grip. I felt that Laure was reduced to a body at that point, I imagined she was not thinking of anything, and I actually felt her escaping my arms, fleeing from the inside by leaving me just her skin, her stiffened muscles, her false heat, so that I felt for the first time that the connection between us was exclusively physical, bestial, based not on attraction but on necessity. I wanted her a bit, to be honest, right then, she was too far away to realize it, or she did not pay attention, hardly the time, she must have been thinking, if she was thinking anything, and I was no longer thinking about anything myself, actually, except for unforeseen details, like how long the doctor would take to get there, but definitely not about me holding Laure tight or, deep down, about me wanting her a few seconds earlier, that was over, the only thing I wanted now was to be warm and alive for her while I waited—as I had waited through the night and as I was still waiting now—for a doctor this time, not waiting for anything from her, I no longer knew anything about her or expected anything of her, of this woman who was escaping me both physically and in her thoughts. I even almost moved away but I told myself I should not, that I owed her this too, to hold her quietly, not knowing a thing.

There were a few seconds of respite, though, when Laure seemed to be appeased and I dipped into sleep before it retracted, slinking back to where it came from, scoffing at my short night. I was beginning to feel tired then, when the telephone rang. At last, I thought. And it was him, the doctor, he was there, the man with the beard informed me, he was coming up.

"Thank you," I said.

I got up to greet him. Laure had started shaking and chattering her teeth again, she could get on with it now, it would not go on for long, someone was coming to stop it.

A bit old perhaps, a bit stooped, but this will do, all the same, I thought.

"Come in," I said.

"Could you wait in the corridor?" he asked me once I had taken him over to the bed, which he would have found anyway, and that made me feel stupid, but it was nothing really, and in fact if he had asked me about her temperature I would not have known. They can sort themselves out on their own, I thought.

Once out on the landing, I waited. I felt as if my life was becoming a modulation of waiting, we had actually got to the point where I was prepared to wait a very long time, and I even began to wonder whether I wanted anything else, whether I should be hoping that my life would be quite simply suspended, and that Laure would not speak again, ever, and that her fever would be succeeded by a silent convalescence, a long bout of passiveness that would not let me get on with anything either, just to wait indefinitely, knowing deep down not to wait for anything anymore, not to envisage doing anything other than staying beside her, in eternal deferment.

And yet there was something that stopped me from wanting to wait there in that corridor. Perhaps because it was the site of that particular brand of waiting, when the doctor might come back out at any moment, and I wanted nothing to do with that sort of waiting, no, I did not want to wait for the doctor, I was not convinced that it was him I was waiting for, it was really Laure, to be honest, and so it irritated me—the corridor did—and I went back down to reception.

The hotelier was there, he often was. He must be someone else who has to settle for waiting, I thought. Not for a client, no, just for life to go by, and perhaps the best way for him to see it passing was to stay at reception with his nose in his book, ever open, then, the book, still the same one. He's a slow reader, I thought, he must linger over every word. I understood that, I often spun books out myself so that every sentence kept its full weight in my memory, or snippets of sentences. Still, the hotelier saw me come down and gave me a wide-eyed look as if, after all those letters, he was adapting to a face, narrowing his pupils, focusing on me.

"Well?" he said.

"I'm waiting," I said.

He did not seem surprised by this admission. But by my being there, yes. He was hardly a talkative man at heart, but his eyes had a great deal to say, at least they did for me, oh yes, this man was talking and what he was now telling me without actually saying it was that I was the one—well, he let slip the suspicion or the question—that I was the one who had made my wife ill, by leaving her alone the night before, and what is more he seemed inclined to confirm this hypothesis because I was down here next to him and not upstairs—behavior that, I felt, he found pretty casual. And, instead of thinking he should mind his own business and not take his nose out of his book to give me that look, I felt compelled to pull myself together for his benefit and find some pretext to cut short this impromptu visit to him so that I could get back upstairs, knowing that—obviously—he could not be deemed to be inducing me to do it, that I could not anchor his expression to some meaning without confirmation of the theory I was putting forward, and that consequently this was my decision alone.

"I think I'd better go back upstairs," I said. "Excuse me."

Back upstairs the corridor was very quiet, then a door opened, but it was not ours. A man appeared and walked past me with his overnight bag to get to the elevator. It was the man from breakfast, who had finally decided to do something, I thought to myself. At the same time I noticed that there were delicate compositions of landscapes evenly spaced along the walls, and it felt as if the hotel were suddenly humanized, there was some warmth in the way it was decorated, and a clientele, even if it was leaving, this clientele, but that was just it, it meant the clientele was normal, and I felt a little less alone.

I did not wait much longer. I had barely started pacing along the corridor when the door to room 25 opened, not strictly speaking leaving room for the doctor to come out, he simply appeared in the gap, leaning half his body out and casting an inquiring glance up and down the corridor. I gathered, from this stance, that he was inviting me to go back into the room with him, and—with my heart full of mixed feelings, subjected to a succession of emotions that never truly contradicted each other though some of them blended together or rather piled on top of each other, as if I were the site of some accumulation, with absolutely no chance of excluding anything at all: anxiety, acceptance, that sinking feeling or just stepping off the edge of a precipice—I went in and he closed the door behind me.

Laure was no longer shaking, she was very calm, lying on her back with her hair clinging to her temples and her eyes, which gazed at the ceiling, surrounded by dark circles I had never seen on her before.

"I've given her an injection," the doctor told me. "She's going to be fine. She needs rest now and medication. She should start the course as soon as possible. It's nothing very serious, believe me, but her whole throat is very badly infected. She mustn't miss a single dose. Call me if there's any problem. Are you staying in the area?"

"Um," I said, and I took out my checkbook.

"Right," he said almost immediately. "I'll get back to my patients."

True enough, Laure was not his patient, she was mine, and once he had left I leaned over her. I did not know what to say to her, right then, right away.

"You need to rest," I decided on. "I'm going to go and get your medicine."

I found it all the easier leaving her because she had given no answer, said nothing, betrayed nothing with a look or a gesture, and by staying longer I might have exposed myself to some reaction on her part, a reaction I feared, just as I feared everything about her since the day before, if the truth be known, to the extent that one cannot rule out the possibility that I was running away, if only temporarily, endowed as I was with the doctor's prescription and a task that could not be postponed: bringing back the medicine. I left and went back past reception, which on this occasion was deserted, not that that was a disappointment to me, I mean, the hotelier was a good enough witness to my life, granted, but the odd pause was no bad thing, I thought, and I wouldn't want to wear the poor man out, you never know.

The pharmacists were there, though, like the day before, and they recognized me. They probably just had good memories for faces, and it was not as if they had crowds of customers anyway, but I had actually only bought some aspirin and a thermometer from them, they could have forgotten that, I thought, or even forgotten me. But no. Worse than that, not satisfied with merely recognizing me, they betrayed no surprise, as if it was normal for people to come back to them after buying aspirin, normal for things to have gotten worse, I mean. They could see I was worried, so they seemed to find it logical that I should come back, logical that I should be worried, and yet there was no trace of compassion in their expression, quite the opposite, there was a sort of ratification of my problem, a serene acceptance of it that felt instantaneous or even, I thought, predated my return. They actually proved very kind, very efficient, like the previous day, in serving me. What is more, they had everything, it was just a slightly larger bag this time, that was all, a slightly larger bag that they filled for me, heavier too, then, even though once again I had the feeling I was carrying something that had no weight, the only difference being that, compared to the day before, I was getting used to this strangeness, to the very singular feeling of transporting pharmaceuticals across a village where I was not so much settling as lingering, like in a transit area where I might wait to be given some sort of passport, some document that would have legitimized me. And that is, in fact, what happened, there, with that prescription, I was doing what I should do, no need for anxiety then, I told myself, everything's quite normal, really.

At the hotel no hotelier. It's a long pause, I thought, I'm being left to cope on my own. I see, I see. I headed back toward room 25, opened the door, and went straight over to Laure who was asleep. I prepared her first doses of antibiotics and expectorants—pill, sachet, glass of water—then I shook her. She woke up.

"Here, take this now," I told her.

She obeyed, without a word at first, then handed back the glass and said:

"Okay, I'm going to sleep, but I'd like you to make your own arrangements, I'd like you to sort yourself out so that you can leave me, I know it's a bit harsh but I want you to go, to go on without me, I really need you not to be here, it's not that I need to be alone, but without you, without you looking at me, without feeling you there, without your questions, without your help, without your care," without your love (she did not add). "I can cope fine on my own" (funny, her too, I thought), "anyway I don't want to go to this birthday, it's a pain, it'll be tiring, I find Philippe tiring, I'm tired."

I had not foreseen that. That she would no longer want to see Philippe. Me, perhaps. But Philippe.

"Don't you want to go?" I asked.

"No."

"What about Philippe?"

"He'll manage without me," she said.

"What about you?"

I realized that I had forgotten to mention myself. I would come to that. In the meantime she said nothing. She really did look tired. She had done far too much talking.

"You're doing far too much talking, anyway," I went on. "What you want, if I've got this straight, is for me to leave you here, ill, at the hotel, three hundred kilometers from home, and then what? What should I be doing if I'm not helping you? What does this mean? How are you going to eat?"

"I'm not hungry," she said. "Don't worry. I'll take care of myself. There are people here."

I thought of the hotelier, yes, except that, if I had to choose, I would say he was closer to me than to her. Not that he would have been incapable of looking after Laure, of course, quite the contrary, well I hardly wanted to go into the whole question of similarities . . .

"So, then, if I left you," I said, "how would you get home? Once you're better."

"By car."

"By car," I echoed. "You would keep the car?"

"Yes," she said. "I would need the car, obviously."

"So then . . ." I said.

She blinked once.

"So then," I went on, "what do I do?"

"You go to Braz," she told me, her voice struggling to overcome my questions, to overcome sleep, to overcome the fever. "You go to Philippe's birthday party. Tonight. You take a train to Quiberon. You find your own way. You do it for me. Now. Please. I've never asked you for anything."

"True," I said.

She was asleep.

I could not get over it. She had asked me for something. And that was to remove myself, of course. Unusual request.

Very unusual.

Right, I said to myself.

I'm going to do just what she wants, I thought. For how many days? God knows. For three days, of course. Why three days? I don't know. Yes I do. Personally, I'm never ill for more than three days. There you have it. Either way, I'll call her. I'll leave the cell phone with her.

Because we had only one cell phone between us, you see. Not to call each other, but for other people. Who called her. And I will call her too, from a phone booth, a bit later. When I have left.

When I have left. There are some eventualities we picture, and others we do not. I could feel the beginnings

of a problem with my eventualities. A problem of impetus, of meaning too. Of direction . . . and yet I did have
one, and I could not envisage any other way of getting
back to Laure.

It is quite a long way, though, I pointed out to
myself.

Quite a journey.

There is Philippe, of course. I had been quite happy
to go to Philippe's house. With her.

Without her, I don't know.

Except.

Without her I don't know what to do, where to go
. . . for her, really. And for me too. For him as well, when
it comes down to it.

Rather than.

I picked up my bag, which had been slumped in the
middle of the room since the day before. I glanced over
at Laure, the woman I love, I told myself. And ill, too. I
really don't want to leave her. I left her.

I did not want to say good-bye to her. I would rather
call her: she would not be able to see me, which might
help her. It would help me.

"Well then?" asked the hotelier, not even waiting for me to show him I was there. He saw me coming, like the pharmacists. "How's it going?"

"Not well," I said.

"It's the first time I've had someone sick in the hotel," he told me. "Confined to bed."

"It's the first time my wife's been sick," I replied. "And that she's confined herself to bed. She's not taking it well. I'm not going to stay."

"Not going to stay where?"

"Here. At the hotel."

"You?" he asked.

"Yes," I said, "me. Not her. She's going to stay. I'd prefer it. She'd prefer it. We'd prefer it."

"So you're leaving, then," the hotelier summarized.

"So I'm leaving, yes," I explained. "I don't know how yet."

He did not seem to understand.

"I'm leaving her the car," I said.

"You're not staying," he said.

"That's right, yes," I said. "No, I'm not staying. She needs me to go."

"Right, well, it's none of my business," said the hotelier. "None at all."

He spread his hands, producing them from nowhere, I had already forgotten where they emerged from: beneath the desk or on top of it. Not from his book, anyway. There was no book on the desk at all. Perhaps he had finished it, the book. He might have been contriving a pause before the next one.

"I'm going to Braz," I explained. "Might there be a train to Quiberon, from Laval? Or even to Vannes?"

Without his book he seemed somehow disarmed. As if he had no references close at hand.

"Yes, there could be," he said eventually. "I don't know anymore. I don't travel now. You could ring the station. You could go back to Le Mans as well. I'll get you the phone book."

Another book, I thought to myself.

"Thank you," I said.

He handed me the phone book, and I leafed through it. I saw nothing, could not see anything, could not find what I wanted. I could not get myself to concentrate.

I closed the phone book and handed it back to him.

"I'm going to go to the station, anyway," I said. "How far is it to Laval?"

"Forty-five kilometers," he said. "If you can get a taxi, that is," he added, laying his hand on the telephone. "If you're not in too much of a hurry. It could take a long time. And be expensive."

He really seemed to be picturing my leaving. Me too. There were two of us, then. Three, even. That was encouraging.

Obviously, he was also putting me in an embarrassing situation. I am not very rich, not even well-off. But then money has never been a problem for me. I do not go out very much. I rarely take two hotel rooms.

He should have been able to see all that.

"I could take you as far as the highway," he said. "It's fifteen kilometers from here."

I thanked him but did not really grasp what he meant. Then I got it: he wanted to take me to the edge of the highway. To leave me there, then. With my thumb in the air, if I had got it right.

Of course it was a long way from who I was, hitchhiking, it went right back to when I was eighteen, and I had to make a considerable effort to establish any sort of link between those days and my present situation. I had an acute feeling of regression.

I wanted to fight it, that feeling. And, in order to fight it, I could find only one thing (incidentally quite a logical thing and, even better, it suggested itself to me there and then): to move forward. Spatially. To turn back as little as possible. Not at all, even. In the first instance.

So I'm leaving Laure, then, I told myself.

For the time being.

"Would you be able to take me now?" I asked him.

He looked up, as if the answer to my question might be inscribed on the top of my head, or a little above it, behind it, on the corridor wall, or toward the foot of the staircase.

"Now, yes," he said. "But I mean right away. Do you have your bag?"

It was at my feet, my bag, but I checked anyway.

"Yes," I said. "Wait," I added. "I'd like to buy a few things."

"What do you mean?"

"For her."

"Oh," he said. "I'll take care of it."

"Thank you," I said. "No meat. If possible."

"Don't worry."

He stood up and walked around the counter.

"Shall we go?"

He was already in front of me and I followed him toward the door, wondering where his car was. There were three cars outside in the parking lot, one of them being mine. But, deep down, it was not so much his car I was trying to imagine as him at the wheel of a car. There was no steering wheel at his counter. No actual wheels either; the whole thing was secured to the floor.

It turned out to be the newest one of the three, the newest car. Well, fancy that. It was air-conditioned. He drove well. We met very little traffic on the D24. In short, we had left. There was cool air coming at my throat. I tilted the ventilation unit downward. I saw three cows.

"There's not much traffic around here," he told me, "but that'll change, you'll see."

I did not know how to reply to this, and he could find nothing to add himself. I think we shared in each other's awkwardness. Which was better than nothing.

People say that in the countryside the kilometers flash by quickly, in a way. A little village with its speed bumps, a bit of a hold-up further on, at a crossroads, and the rest is just trees, fields, two roundabouts with a cart full of flowers in the middle or something—anything—figurative or perhaps abstract, something that catches your eye just long enough for you to turn your head . . . and we were there. We did not even have time to think. Well, it went quickly for me, anyway. Very quickly. I would have liked to exchange a few words with my host, at least. I will have to accept that it was not possible. We were straight on to the good-byes.

"Right," he said, holding out his hand to me.

"Thanks again," I said.

I had not moved from my seat. The highway was there, I could see it, we were beside it, no longer completely perpendicular to it, beyond the red light, around the bend. Opposite us was a shop full of lights and leather chairs.

"Would you be able to take me a little farther?" I asked.

"No, no," he said. "You're in the shopping area, here. Lots of people stop here, look."

"I can see," I said. "But I'd prefer to stop them for myself."

He must have found me complicated.

"Whatever you want," he said. "I'll take you another kilometer farther on."

"Thank you."

Another kilometer farther on they were no longer selling chairs. Cars were no longer parking. There were no red lights either. It was back to the fields again. We were a long way beyond the service station. There was nothing, in fact. Just the highway. And me. And no phone booths.

I fiddled with my phone card in my pocket. I did not register, in my immediate vicinity, a single human presence. The cars hurtling right past me were very probably inhabited, but their drivers were faceless. In fact I started by ignoring them, uneasy about clarifying the situation, particularly the reasons that had brought me to this, alone, on the edge of this road, fiddling with my phone card.

It was actually difficult to make the connection. In any event, I was here. And I needed to call Laure, at least to tell her that I was no longer there, that she should not worry about not seeing me at her bedside. About seeing me there, sorry. I was just afraid I might wake her when I called. It would be better to wait.

I had no choice, mind you. Commercy, the little town that the hotelier had helped me get past, was a long way off now with its phone booths. Or its phone booth. Which might be out of order, too. Anyway, retracing my steps was not a possibility. I had a journey to undertake, in a specific direction. I would call Laure farther on, later, when the time was right.

Oh well, I thought to myself. Come on, then. Give them a sign. You have to do it. Stop looking at the scenery, I can't believe this. There isn't any scenery. Those fields over there look like any other field. There isn't even any rape to make a contrast, and it's nowhere near a patchwork. No picturesque swaying in that wheat field. I say wheat, but I don't know what it is. I don't give a damn. I will gladly acknowledge that there is some sky, though. A beautiful big blue sky with clouds, the whole thing very clear and distinct, and warm, not too warm, thanks to that breeze stirring. Or which has stirred, I don't really know. Perfect weather. And me, then, watching the streams of cars. Deafened, drunk on it, whipped by the displaced air. Still with my bag in my hand. I can't seem to put it down.

Yes I can, I put it down. The sort of guy who cannot go on like that. With too much on his hands. He lifts an arm. The sort of guy who asks for help. From no one in particular. And who doesn't do it for the fun of it: he doesn't find this fun. He'd much rather be somewhere else. That's just it. He'd really like someone to take him somewhere else.

He's a man in difficulty, relatively speaking. He's not going to die. Well dressed, too, decent. He's obviously here by chance. The movement with his arm isn't quite right. Well, it is. It's on the inside that it seems stilted, but from the outside you can't fault it: the forearm is supple, the thumb is up. At first he tried a different form of signaling—in vain. A closed fist puts people off. An open palm irritates them. All that's left is the classic gesture, then, and he masters it as well as the next man.

He's getting used to it, even. He can go one better than that: he's tiring of it. It only took him half an hour. So he's got the hang of it. Now he's going to start worrying, trying to find a way out . . . not right away. He sneezes first and, for a moment, he's lost in that sneeze. It must be the breeze, or the pollen, he can never tell what sets it off, doesn't try to. Has got used to that, yup. He blows his nose.

It's his cold. His, coming back. Not really full strength, just a reminder. Maybe it's also because he's on his own, he needs something to do. He blows his nose and someone stops. Thirty meters beyond him. No logical connection between these two things. He finishes blowing his nose, the car looks like the hotelier's, he thinks it is the hotelier, if the hotelier's coming back—like the cold—then he must be coming to get him, because he needs to go back, him, because it's better to go back, get back to the hotel, now . . . but it's not the hotelier. It's not his car. It's basically the same model, but a different make. He picks up his bag, sets off, I'm setting off, then, I say to myself, because this is what she wanted, and I've actually left, I'm on my way, I'm holding myself to this because I need to hold myself together, to hold on, I cover the thirty meters, the driver has lowered the passenger window.

"Where are you going?"

"To Laval. I don't know if"

"If what? Get in."

I opened the door. The man was wearing a short-sleeved shirt, not me, I need full-length sleeves, I mean. He was smiling. No, no that is wrong, it was me. He was sad, or serious. Exactly as if he had something to do and was not enjoying this but there it was. When you have to. He looked uncomfortable. But I was not forcing his hand: I only blew my nose.

So it was me, then, the smile. I thanked him, he had put me in a good mood, all of a sudden, he was helping me, and he had not stopped for nothing. He took my bag, put it on the rear seat and set off.

"I'm not going all the way to Laval," he said. "I'll get you a bit farther on, though. Does that help, if I get you a bit farther on?"

I was asking myself the same question.

"It looks like that's a problem," he went on. "I'm sorry. But I really don't have time to go all the way to Laval. Maybe I shouldn't have picked you up."

"I don't know," I said. "Could you drop me near a phone booth? I need to call someone."

"Use my cell phone."

He pointed to the side pocket.

"No, thanks," I said. "Drop me here. I need to find another car, anyway. I'm wasting time like this."

He looked uncomfortable, over and above his uncomfortable look. I have no better way of saying it.

"I would gladly have stayed with you a bit longer," I said. "When you've been so kind. But you see it's me who's. I'm missing cars."

He was wearing a tie. Not just a short-sleeved shirt. Drove well . . . but what was the point of that, he was absolutely no use to me. He irritated me. I was not in a good mood now.

He slowed down. A hundred meters farther on there was a lay-by; he stopped there.

"There you are," he announced without cutting the engine. "But you could just as easily have called from my house. I'll be there in ten minutes. You could have a coffee, take your time, make your call, and I'll take you on to Laval. I'll have a bit of time, afterward. But not now. I've got frozen food in the trunk."

"If you can take me to Laval," I said, "fine."

He must have appreciated my generosity of spirit. I could feel him relaxing at the thought of helping me. Of course, all this implied that I should make some sort of conversation with him, but I did not feel like tackling any major subjects. To do with myself, at least. I was quite happy to talk about the war—there was a war, not that far away.

"I wouldn't have thought of the frozen food," I said. "Obviously."

We set off again. He nodded. I understood what he meant. I was thinking about Laure, or I should say about me. I wondered who I was, here, now. I could not see clearly what lay ahead for me.

"I'm having a birthday party this evening," he said. "My name's Gilles."

He held out his hand.

"Pleased to meet you," I said. "That's funny."

"Excuse me?"

"Nothing," I said. "How old will you be?"

Thirty five. He looked older. Maybe it was the tie. Or the serious expression. The countryside was changing now, we were going through some woods, in the shade for a while. I could not make myself see him as a young man.

"You haven't told me your name."

"Serge."

I took the first name that came to me. Serge was actually a sort of friend. Who was very unlikely to meet Gilles. No one was likely to meet him, even I was there by chance. It was also by chance that Gilles was celebrating his birthday. Ah well, I said to myself. All the same. All the same. But, in a way, that was nothing to do with it. He was almost a different generation. A different world. Only the countryside maintained any kind of connection. There were still trees, then fields again, and farms. A village.

"We're here," he said.

He stopped near the church and we got out. There was a doorway in a windowless wall, well, that was how I saw it; I identified some windows later. Gilles was holding his bag of frozen food, and I my bag of clothes. He rang the bell and a woman opened the door.

"Serge," he said. "My wife, Hélène."

He was not really good enough for her. I could not make them out. When people are welcoming like that it becomes difficult. You see yourself, answer their questions, amaze yourself—you would never have thought of it: me, for example, and having Laval as a destination. The importance it takes on.

"You could just call to get the train times," suggested Hélène.

"I know," I said. "Thank you."

The importance it takes on for other people. Having to get there, to Laval. When in fact. I waited for more questions.

"Shall I make you a coffee?"

"I'd love one, thank you."

We were in a sort of corridor. Parallel to the garden, with French windows. A charming garden, surrounded by a low wall. A little pond. A big tree in the middle. Half dead, it looked to me. I could only see its light-colored trunk, ravaged by mistletoe.

It was not actually a corridor, although it did lead to a living room to the left and a kitchen to the right. There was a table pushed up against the wall, opposite the windows. The house had probably not always been a house. An agricultural building, I imagined. I could have been standing in the place where they used to tie up cattle. There was a metal ring embedded in the wall.

"You stay there," Hélène told me. "I'm going to make the coffee."

She pointed to the table and drew out a chair from beneath it. I would have preferred moving from there. I was very happy to have a break, but feeling I was settling in, no. I found it embarrassing.

"Can I help you?"

I followed Hélène into the kitchen. Gilles was already in there, grappling with his freezer. The worktops on either side of the sink were covered in cans, packets, serviettes, chopping boards, bowls of fruit, various kinds of bread, and a great pile of cheeses.

"That's very kind but you really shouldn't bother, you don't know where anything is. But come on, come in."

I came to a halt somewhere to the right of the sink, looking up and down the work surface. I skimmed a packet of potato chips with my fingers, almost as if feeling the fabric of a drape. It rustled. I drew my hand away immediately.

Hélène, who was busy with the coffeemaker, did not pay any attention to me. I could just as easily not have been there or, conversely, could have been there for ages, a few hours, or a few days, I found it hard to evaluate. I felt a sort of doubt, nothing much, but it weighed me down. I felt like getting rid of it by sharing it with the others.

"Do we know each other?" I asked. "Have we ever met?"

"I don't think so," Hélène replied, pressing the button on the coffeemaker. "Are you from around here?"

"No," I said. "Obviously," I added. Of course.

I did not know these people, no. They were just familiar, that was all. I drank my coffee, alone, while Hélène attended to her preparations. It was big, their house, I did not get in the way of their comings and goings, and they did not seem bothered by my presence.

They stepped around me. Even their questions, when it came down to it, avoided touching me. They flitted around me peripherally.

"Don't you want to call the station? Would you like me to do it?"

It was always Hélène, not getting rid of me but worrying about me. No personal worries at all, I noticed, just simple concern for others. She was almost beautiful, when I looked at her. But I did not look at her.

"It's really very kind but I'd rather just go there, and see the timetables when I'm there. I really like stations. Spending a bit of time at stations."

"Are you on vacation?"

She was taking an interest in me. Or she was having a taste to see what I was, as if I were part of some buffet, something tricky to identify on the plate. I was not really sure. It hardly seemed to matter much, anyway.

Gilles left us, carrying some glasses out on a tray. Handing me over, I imagined. Someone was taking care of me, that was all that mattered. To him, I mean.

"You could see it like that," I said.

I would have been very happy to be on vacation. I did not have much to do. Waiting till the time was right to make my call, taking a train, not leaving for it too late. Or perhaps not taking it. I had the choice, there. There was a woman somewhere who was not coming with me, my woman to be precise, and had left me grappling with time. And with space too. I was like an insect. I would have preferred a straight line.

I did not know, to be honest, whether I would go to Braz. Not yet. Not entirely.

"Could I use your cell phone? I have to call a cell, actually."

It was midday. I borrowed Gilles's cell phone and dialed the number for our cell, Laure's and mine. I got the messaging service. I had recorded the announcement.

It really was me, then. Almost as if it were me, there, apologizing for her absence. I did not have the heart to contradict myself. I did not want to upset myself. I did not leave a message.

My hosts had left me in the living room, concerned that I should make this intimate call alone. I thought of going back to join them, of helping, but Hélène had discouraged me from doing that. I looked at my watch, gave myself a quick half hour before calling back. When it comes down to it, waiting is a perfectly coherent position.

It was my position, anyway, and my only problem was furnishing it. I went out and walked around the garden. It suited me fine, walking along the walls—for a while, at least. My hosts, who I could see through the kitchen window, glanced out at me from time to time. I regularly slipped out of sight for them, then reappeared. I had already been around a few times. A thought came to me: I could go out into the street, go and have a look at the church, but I did not dare. I was afraid my hosts might worry if I went too far. Even if I did not take my bag. They had asked me in, and I hesitated to step through their door in the opposite direction.

I did not know them well enough, in fact. I was not bothering them, but they were me. A little. I would have felt happier being alone at their house. Ideally. Walking around in circles without being seen. That is what I would have done at the station, if I had gone there. It is true that Gilles had offered to drive me there. He had brought his frozen food home, okay. I had not yet made my call. Thank goodness time kept passing, inevitably.

I called again. Laure picked up. Her voice was not the same. What I mean is that it was back to being the same, the same as before. Or nearly. Nasal, of course, but self-possessed. A little too self-possessed. She was not feeling so bad.

"What sort of not so bad?" I asked. "Do you still have a temperature? Are you still shaking?"

"I'm okay," she said. "Better. I'm tired. How about you?"

"Me?" I said.

I had not been expecting that question. I preferred not to tell her I was at someone else's house, still not heading anywhere.

"I'm at the station in Laval," I said.

I realized that she had not asked me where I was, not specifically at least. I could just as easily have told her I was fine. Or that I was not, even. Mind you, I still could tell her that: things are not great, not great at all. I'm at the station in Laval and I'm feeling terrible. I miss you.

"Hello?" she said.

"Can you get up?" I asked. "Are you in bed?"

"Yes."

"Can you get up?"

"I suppose so, yes."

"Couldn't you come and join me? Come and pick me up?"

"Drive?" she asked.

"Don't feel like it," she answered herself.

"Don't feel like what?" I asked.

"Don't feel like anything."

"Right," I said. "What are you going to do?"

"I don't know."

"Are you going home?"

"Yes."

"When?"

"I don't know."

"What are we going to do?" I said.

"I don't know," she said.

"Well, I'll call you again then," I said. "Big kiss."

"Okay."

"You don't want to give me a kiss," I said.

"Yup."

She hung up. What am I doing? I asked myself. My nose tickled. My nose tickled again. Let's just keep on sneezing, I thought. Let's start with a sneeze at least.

I sneezed seven times in a row. I had not done that for a year. I have already said that I had been living with a low-level cold for a year, a simple nasal congestion not punctuated by more serious bouts. Now, contrary to what such a habitus might lead one to suspect, I loathe sneezing. Sneezing does not agree with me. Granted, I can derive some pleasure from the first sneeze. The second is acceptable. But a sequence of the things exasperates me . . . that feeling that it will never end.

On the other hand, I have also already said that it gives you something to do. That remains a good aspect of the situation. And it was one way of responding to Laure. In her absence, which I struggled with so ineffectually, I was not displeased to have to battle with myself. To take a bit of an interest in myself. That is the advantage of a minor ailment, it gives you some sort of structure. Even so, it can be misleading: the time always comes when it dies down.

My fit of sneezing took place in the garden. I might have been seen, from the windows. Personally, I have never seen anyone sneeze from a distance. I do not know, without the sound cut out, what sort of effect it would give. That slight spasm. Seven times over. That sort of paradoxical head-nodding, which is the very opposite of acquiescence.

I could see them busying themselves, through the windows. Now that I was feeling better, I wondered whether I should go back to join them. They were not expecting me, but they had made me welcome, all the same. They had invited me. Mind you. I felt happier staying out there alone for the time being. I walked around the garden, yet again. Laure was feeling better. I, therefore, could not understand why she did not want to come and join me. Let us consider that I did not want to understand. I could choose not to call her back. But I would rather just do it.

Except that I did not have Gilles's cell phone with me. I went into the house.

"Is there really nothing I can do to help?"

"There is actually. We're going to set the table. Will you stay for lunch?"

That was Hélène. She seemed to think I was in no hurry to leave. Personally, I did not really know what to think of it.

"Why not?" I said.

It would give me a bit of time. But I did not know whether I needed time. I needed to call Laure back.

Hélène seemed to want me to join in, she was handing me plates. I took them.

"Could I use your phone again?"

"It's on the table."

Which I was supposed to be setting. I laid out the plates by guesswork, on three sides of the rectangle. Then I moved over toward the windows and dialed our number.

"It's me," I said.

"Yes."

"Don't you want to see me?"

"No."

"You don't love me anymore."

"You exaggerate everything."

"I'm not exaggerating anything. I miss you."

"Fine."

"I just don't recognize you," I explained.

"Well, I do," she said. "I need to."

"Can you explain?"

"No."

"I could come back," I said. "Back to the hotel. And we could go home to Paris. We won't go to the party."

"Are you not on the train?"

"Yes. Nearly."

"It's tonight," she said.

"I know."

"I'm glad you're going. Really."

"Really glad?"

"Yes. That you're going. Really."

I did not press the point.

"Without you," I said, "it feels weird."

It was not exactly the word I was looking for.

"I'd like you to give him a big hug from me," she said.

"I've never hugged him," I pointed out, as we were changing the subject. "And I was going with you."

"You're wearing me out," she said. "I'm going to hang up."

"I'll call you later."

"Fine."

"Big kiss."

I was not getting any better at this. She had hung up. I could not get used to the woman's absence. To her being away from me. To what she was stopping me from being: with her. Without her, obviously, I had a clear field . . . like a desert.

"The cutlery," I said, "is it in this drawer?"

Hélène was not far away. She was busy with lunch. Big day, I thought, for these people. And me here, looking like I'm not doing anything. When in fact.

"Oh, please," Hélène reassured me, "don't feel that you have to help, Serge. We're on a roll now. Sit yourself down."

Serge. Right, well, I did not have the heart to contradict her. To explain that, even though I was called Serge, I would rather people did not call me that. Especially so soon. In a way, of course, it helped. Other people being so sure. The way they filled the vacuum.

We ended up sitting at the table. I felt I owed them some conversation. At the very least, it was my duty to do the meal justice. I forced myself to proceed by sampling a little of their assorted vegetables, flanked by chicken breast. As for a subject that I might have been able to tackle without too much effort, it would obviously be Gilles's birthday. Given that it was his birthday, Gilles's.

Gilles and Philippe.

Serge and me.

As for Laure, she was the only one who needed no one else to become two different people.

"Are you expecting a lot of guests this evening?" I asked them.

There, I was proving that I took an interest in their plans. In their party. Not knowing where anything went and having not sent out any invitations myself, I felt rather uncomfortable in the position—the median position—I had taken in their day. I tried to project myself into their evening, but discreetly, given that I had not been invited. As for wishing Gilles a happy birthday there and then, I felt I had no right to. Unless I could think of myself as a guest who had arrived very early, which was not the case. I was neither a guest nor early. Nor late. Either way, it was not the time.

Nevertheless I was there. And the two of them continuously administered proof of the fact.

"We're expecting a dozen or so friends," said Gilles. "You could have stayed, in fact, you'd be very welcome. But you wouldn't know anyone, and you have to go, anyway. We're not trying to get rid of you, of course."

I was touched. Embarrassed, too. Not so much by this proposition that rode roughshod over my sense of propriety than by the complication it introduced into my choices. Besides, it was not really a proposition. Well, it might only have taken one word, even one slightly hesitant look on my part for it to be consolidated.

But I had not blinked. I had taken a second helping from the dish as a way of repaying their kindness, duly attributing this quality to both of them. Yes, I did have to go. I really did have to exist a little for them, even if only out of courtesy. I already had a name, all I had to do was act as if there was someone behind it. By the same token, this was now forcing me to hit the road again.

Even if Laure changed her mind and delivered me from this detour. In which case I would set off again in the opposite direction. But I was afraid to call her now, afraid of suffering. I was paralyzed, my thoughts kept getting blocked, and—in physical terms—I would have been completely incapable of getting to my feet. I was reduced to jaws, palate, throat, and swallowing. And at what a price! I was finding it harder and harder to eat.

Not that this was of great concern: we were coming to the end of the meal. But I had no desire for it to be the end of anything.

Right. I imagine that, deprived of all plans, not even having the excuse of some job to do, my immobility now, as the end of this meal—rather slowly—took shape, was beginning to look like a sort of petrification on my part, and I was left with no other solution than to stir myself from the inside. So then I sneezed yet again, hoisted sharply from my chair and falling back down on to it (not from a very great height, true), armed with a hankie that I had produced like an illusionist, thanks to a maneuver that—although probably planned on the outer reaches of my conscience—left me in a state of wonderment. I did have to stand up, though, in anticipation of another spasm, which soon gripped me and to which I surrendered with some poise, yes, but deploying the particular restraint that I believe some of us are capable of displaying and that consists in giving in while emitting only the most furtive sound, the sort that—if you were hidden in a damp thicket patrolled by hostile guards—it would be best to be able to produce in order to avoid being caught.

Gilles and Hélène were watching me, still sitting at the table and not daring to start clearing it, I imagine, as they waited for another paroxysm from me, and certainly indecisive as to what would be an appropriate response. So I sneezed again, then, perfecting my method, although keen to move away now so that I could get through my crisis in relative privacy, without being able to exert any further control over myself. I apologized, went out to the garden, and hid as best I could to give in to my pantomime. Then I came back into the house, exhausted and with my nostrils burning.

"You're not well," Hélène commented.

They were both there waiting for me, by the door into the garden.

"It'll pass," I said. "It always does eventually."

"Don't you want to lie down?" Hélène suggested. "It'll be quiet upstairs."

She tilted her nose—hers that was perfectly dry—toward the stairs.

"I was thinking of helping you."

From their embarrassed expressions I could see that they did not know what to get me to do. My position was growing clearer: I was becoming a burden. And, lying down upstairs, I would certainly not have been in their way so much.

"We're going back to work in the kitchen," Hélène explained. "Gilles and me. Sit yourself down in the living room with a book, if you prefer. What are you going to decide, about your train?"

"In fact," I ventured, "I don't really feel like going where I'm going. But I'm not committed."

I needed to get out of this embarrassing situation and, anyway, I owed it to them to confide in them a bit, when all was said and done. All the same, they looked shocked.

"I'm in a situation where I'm really not sure what to do," I explained to them. "I'm so sorry. You've met me at a strange time."

I held myself in check to avoid saying more. Except that it was already quite a lot, I felt. Not just for them.

"And you're not feeling well, either," Hélène reminded us all.

"True," I said. "I think I'm coming down with a really bad cold on top of everything else. And I might as well tell you that, even if I left now, I'd arrive too late."

That was what I had just realized. Even if there were still a train to take me to Quiberon at that time of day, there would not be a boat to get me to Braz that evening. So I would not be seeing Philippe on his birthday.

Later, I told myself. Tomorrow.

Bad luck for Philippe.

Bad luck for Laure.

But I would go.

To have somewhere to go.

Not to come back.

Right there and then I could not see myself coming back.

That was the point, in fact: I could not see myself. Not in that sense. In the other sense, I came across as a sort of silhouette. An outline.

"Is it serious?" Hélène asked.

"No," I reassured her. "An invitation. Just an invitation. It's not very important."

"If I've got this right," Gilles intervened, "you're free."

"Not exactly," I explained. "Let's say things are getting clearer."

That must have sounded vague to them.

"Do you have somewhere to live?" Gilles asked me. "Do you want to make any more calls? Can we do something?"

"You're very kind," I thanked them. "If you could take me to the station whenever it suits you, I'll see how I get on."

"But now that you're not going . . ." Gilles said.

"I'm going to have to go some day," I pointed out to him.

"In your state," Hélène intervened, "you shouldn't move for now."

"I'm holding up your preparations," I said.

"Actually there is something that you could do," she said. "Well, I don't know, I'm only saying this because it seems like you don't really want to go but at the same time you keep wanting to help. So, you see, I was just wondering whether you could drive, now."

"Um," I said.

"No," she said. "It's a stupid idea."

"But I could," I protested. "I could drive, of course I could. Just tell me where."

"You could go and pick up the cake," she suggested.

They were very trusting to lend me their car. I could have been anyone. I wondered, in passing, what Serge would have done in my shoes (he had been drifting in and out of my thoughts ever since his name came to me). Obviously, he would not have gone off with the car. Without coming back, I mean. Serge was like me, like us, averagely honest.

It was certainly diverting thinking about him when, not really knowing who I was dealing with, I was avoiding contact with myself.

Except with respect to honesty, Serge was, alas, not at all like me. He was someone I saw very little, in fact, because he lived alone and, since I had been living with Laure, he probably preferred meeting me without her. Anyway, I had never lived alone. I would see Serge during my breakups. He tackled his existence to the inverse rhythm, trying himself out at love in off-peak periods. He was constantly busy with his various activities, living life like a tourist while I felt that I was inhabiting my life.

A bit lightweight, then, Serge. Running headlong toward his fate with his nose either up in the air or buried in his diary. Whereas I had never played with time, every day considering the next to be an insuperable problem, not to mention the day itself, of course, which I took on bodily and so seriously, with an earnestness that sometimes made Laure laugh. When it did not worry her, of course.

I kept thinking about her. Could not stop thinking about her. About her love. About her kind of love. Where and how it managed to creep in, when it was that particular type of love. Or perhaps it was not a type, it was a phase. A bottleneck, a narrowing. Her love had curled itself up very small, that was all. Taking this opportunity, before resuming its usual dimensions, to assume a type, in fact. It really should not have bothered. The pointlessness of it, the danger of coquetry in that department. If I wanted to I could write a book about all that. About the vanity of putting it on like greasepaint, wearing love like stage makeup. Dressing it up, fine, but . . .

The truth was that I did not have anything. Not anything about anything. Laure would not tell me anything. Refused to. I had no chance of understanding. I had never had the opportunity to understand, in fact. And, now that things were becoming especially incomprehensible, I wanted to understand. I knew that there was no point, but I cannot help it, it is instinctive. Everyone knows that. She does too. So then.

So then, there is dignity. At the end of the day, the end of the road, when all else is lost. I was not at the end of the road: I had just been held up. Unavailable. Burdened by what Laure was refusing from me, and which was weighing on me.

It did not stop me from doing something. Or it drove me to do something. That was just it. Better to move about, under the circumstances. To avoid getting stuck in the mud.

I had accepted the mission entrusted to me. Gilles had shown me the dashboard, the levers, the gearshift, it only took him a few seconds but, before that, I had wanted to reassure my hosts that I was trustworthy, and that had taken longer. I wanted to leave not only my bag—taking it with me would have been unimaginable, anyway—but also my wallet. I had relieved myself of it discreetly, leaving it in an obvious place on the kitchen table. Not too obvious, so that they did not notice it right away. But the space between obvious and the mitigation of it was so slight that it was only a matter of seconds before Hélène brought the thing back to me on the doorstep —and, for a moment, I wondered whether it was so that I could pay for the cake, but it did not last long, my thoughts very quickly turned to something else.

Firstly, in fact, to going to the baker's shop. It was the first idea that came to me, and the most accessible as well. Mentally at least, geographically it was quite a different matter.

I got lost, probably a wrong turning. I only just missed a slip road that would have taken me back to Paris. I parked near a tobacconist's opposite a church, the one in Bourgoin, and I asked the man behind the counter the way to the baker. It was not on the other side of the world, it turned out. The shop was just there, beyond the Shell station. You could park outside if you rode up on the sidewalk. It had just opened up again, there was already a line of people. I wondered where they could all be coming from.

The three salesgirls kept my mind busy. I had to go all the way to Bourgoin to find a baker's shop so completely saturated with sex. The oldest of them, who was at the till, was the most sensual, red lips, lingering looks, curvaceous hips beneath a skirt that the imagination said was very short behind the counter. I never actually knew. She never moved away from it, the counter. Her skirt could just as easily have revealed no more than her ankles, but that is not what we imagined, it was beyond our strength. (What I mean is there were probably several of us thinking that she was doing it on purpose.) There were a few men here, among the women. As for the other two salesgirls—young, pretty as pictures—they had complementary attributes: tall, short, dark, blond, with contrasting outfits that completed this effect of distancing them from each other, as if they were at opposite extremities of a world that intended people to trail from one end of it to the other in order to come up with those two girls. I am barely exaggerating, I have never understood the meaning of their being there like that, together. It was impossible to imagine them going home after work, or it was but together, like interdependent elements of an incendiary device stowed in a box.

I say this because it was a baker's shop, in a perfumery I might not have noticed. But it was well and truly a baker's shop, with the smell (I had to imagine, not having my nose), and the ballet of those two girls between the till and the wicker racks, not to mention the dark-haired one's excursion into the back shop to get fresh bread, the trip there and back, of course, quite logically walking away with her back to me and inevitably coming back facing me, bending at the waist over the large basket, coming back up with an armful of loaves, transferring them onto the racks while the floor tiles clicked under the heels of this harvesting beauty with her made-up eyes. With the waiting, obviously, it is eventually your turn. It was mine.

I stood facing the woman on the till whose lips I now discovered, and the blond girl who asked me what I would like. To have a clearer idea of what was going on! I could have answered, to be less disoriented or just to understand the meaning of my disorientation, which circle of which cocoon-like brand of hell I was in, here and everywhere else, what it is that life has been trying to tell me since yesterday evening, why it keeps lavishing care on me when it seems clear these attentions are not intended for me because I don't benefit from them, that I wasn't a good choice for all this. Serge might have made something of it, him with his lack of strategy, but not me, I'm sorry, I don't want any of it, any of what people are offering me or what they pretend to be offering me—oh, except, I've actually come to pick up an order for Mr. and Mrs. Traverse. I've come a long way to do it, too. I've had quite a journey coming to get this cake.

The blonde undulated away toward a table full of cardboard boxes closed over with flaps, and she consulted the felt-tip inscriptions on them. I tried to tell myself she was looking after me, that she was thinking about my personal case, and that was also what people in the line behind me could have been thinking, especially as her searching—which she carried out rather slowly, to be honest—threatened to exasperate them, as could the small of her back that, because of the way she was standing, looked especially lovely as she leaned over. And I actually viewed myself from that exterior perspective, making two of myself the better to see us, the salesgirl and me, or at least to see myself seeing her serving me, but I stayed on the periphery of this, standing there on my side of the counter, not really thinking of anything (which, I have to admit, was already an improvement), while the salesgirl came back over to me, lifting the flap of the box to show me the cake.

"Is it this one?" she asked me. And, dropping my gaze from her kohl-lined eyes to look at the cake, I was surprised to find myself looking into another pair of eyes, a pair of eyes watching me from the surface of the cake, because it was in fact the cake that was looking at me now and that, amazingly enough, allowed me to identify it as Mr. and Mrs. Traverse's order, because those eyes looking at me from the cake, from the iced surface of the cake, were Gilles Traverse's, whose face, I realized, was reproduced in edible form, actually covering the cake in a layer of icing probably taken from a photo provided by Hélène Traverse, so that the moment the salesgirl showed me the cake I knew that it was the right one, giving me a sudden feeling of being in control, and I was able to confirm it for her.

Then, just before the blonde closed the box back up, I returned briefly to my eye contact with Gilles Traverse, and realized that I had not properly looked at him before but here he was, glimpsed quickly, incarnate, metamorphosed in film. I also noted that, despite his fragile appearance, he was here to affirm his existence, if only ephemerally, but that did not matter: Gilles Traverse was creating his exact double, or—to be more precise— replicating himself, thereby reinforcing the vividness of his very being. And so it was with great caution that I now carried him out to the car (having taken out my wallet but been told that the order had been paid for), so that his skin did not crack, holding him absolutely horizontal. So much so that, as I set off, I had even forgotten the sales-girls, or rather they were now melting into the combined effect they created with the cake, my hosts, and this day in my life that, despite its incoherence, was populated with figures, faces, and places, providing me with a set of reference points that failed to guide me but with whose help I at least managed to move about, even if I did have the obscure impression of being lost.

So I did set off on my return trip then, but as I came into the Traverses' village and even drew level with their house—perhaps because I was retracing my steps, inter-rupting or even in some way contradicting the distanc-ing process to which I had been prey since the day before, clearly backtracking in fact—I was actually heading back toward the hotel. Although I had been commissioned to run an errand and was now responsible for the delicate reproduction of my host (which I needed to deliver to him so that their party could have its full meaning for everyone), the thought of Laure kept haunting me, as did the need to know what she was doing without me, as did the fear of knowing.

I was not seriously thinking about seeing her, no. Going back to the hotel, yes (given that I was on my way) . . . and seeing, then. But perhaps not her, no. The hotelier, in a pinch. Or probably not. No one. Just the hotel.

In the meantime, I thought about justifying the delay to the Traverses, and that gave me an opportunity to propagate my anxiety. Luckily it was not my car so I was constrained to take certain precautions that also stopped me from thinking too much. Most of the time, if the truth be known, I was not thinking. I settled for looking for the road that would get me back to the hotel. I found it, even, and traveled through the countryside backward, which was not very different—different enough, mind you, for me to get lost again, but not too lost, just five or six kilometers in the wrong direction and back again, then I reached the highway where I had been found with my thumb in the air by the man whose cake I was transporting and whose car I was driving, the same car he had invited me into and in which, I remember, he had been transporting frozen food. Viewed from the outside, we had some points in common but that is where the similarities ended: despite these borrowed trappings, my life was taking its own course and, actually, I am the one who is sneezing, now, I told myself, I alone, after that long period of respite in front of the girls at the bakery, and I hung onto the steering wheel, no way could I swerve. Anyway, I had arrived.

And, in the same way that it was very much my cold, it was also very much my hotel, the one I had left that morning. Our car was no longer there. I parked in the space it had vacated and, before getting out of the driver's seat, waited for confirmation of the predicted cascade of sneezes that had announced their arrival as I passed the village sign. I gave in to them and, as anticipated, they took control of me, thrusting me forward against the useful protection of my seat belt, that I had not yet undone, so that it blocked the end of each spasm and stopped me knocking into the steering wheel, bringing me back to reality each time, so to speak safe and sound, as I straightened myself up, still flailing, and kept my eyes glued to the front porch of the hotel through the windscreen.

I blew my nose, pushed open the car door, stepped up to the entrance of the hotel and then to the reception

desk where the hotelier still sat, unaltered and unalter-
able, still reading. When he heard me he looked up from
the book as if I had been the next line, suddenly exiled
from the page that he marked carefully. Perhaps, I told
myself, he did that because—as far as he is concerned—
I am just a digression, a rather slow passage that he would
be happy to skim over before picking up the thread again.
What he did not appear to know, or he pretended not to
know, was that he too was just a passage to me, that I was
skimming over him in the same offhand way, with the
exception that I noticed, I took the time to notice, that
he had hardly changed since this morning, that he was
exactly the same man, barely any older, I thought, a little
bit more slumped though, as if the few hours that separated us, having failed to whiten his beard, had manifestly
performed their duties. Or perhaps it was just me, feeling
as if time had been dilated to the extreme since the morning . . . none of which alters the fact that I had come back
to him as if recovering from a blinding light, focusing on
his face, not surprised to see him again but approaching
him now as if at the end of a parenthetical clause.

"Hello," I said. "If I'm not mistaken, my wife has
gone out. I can't see the car."

The hotelier nodded, apparently relieved that the anticipated digression should prove so brief, although not actually going back to his book, no.

"She left a good hour ago now," he replied, "with her luggage."

"Did she say anything to you?" I asked him.

I was well aware that I was making the man work when he had nothing to do with all this but, well, if Laure had not said anything to him he could just say no, and if that was not the case then it was not particularly difficult either, he only had to repeat what she had said, she had done all the work for him. Either way, the way he hesitated made me think that she had told him something he was not sure he should repeat to me. But no:

"Nothing in particular," he told me. "I didn't know what to do," he added, "I was worried about you."

"That's very kind," I thanked him, "but I don't see what you could have done. How did she seem?"

"Like someone who was leaving," he replied, "pretty friendly, she had a bit of a cold but nothing like as bad as yours," he said. "That's all she's left you."

"What?" I said. "Oh," I realized. "Never mind, I have to go."

"You'd do better to sit down for a bit," he said, attempting to hold me up. "Sit yourself down for a while, you're not well, it's obvious, you've got quite a nose, you could easily stay here to think, all my rooms are free, you can take whichever one you like, it's on the house. The way things are going for me . . ." he said, coming out from behind the counter.

I would have preferred it if he had stayed sitting down.

"Listen," I said, "I'm very touched by your offer," and at that moment his wife appeared.

"Ah," she said, "it's the man from number 29, so you came back," she said to me.

She came over to join us and all three of us stood in the foyer, without witnesses—I could just as easily have killed them, it was too many people to talk to, suddenly, too much concern, I felt a searing desire to be with myself again, to erase these people standing facing me like a sub-clause, because *they* were the sub-clause, not me, even their hotel was just a sub-clause, a hiatus in time with a blurred interior, unworkable.

"Listen," I told them, "I actually have to go, someone's expecting me, I'm in a hurry. Thank you for everything."

And I left them behind. I felt selfish, but I did have my own commitments. I do what I can, I told myself. And now, I went on, I'm going to stop at a phone booth to call Laure, and I'm going to call her, this time she's going to have to tell me something. That she's left, at least. And I found the phone booth at the highway crossroads where the hotelier had driven me. And I called her. Messaging service. Obviously, I thought. If she's driving. She's on the freeway now.

Not for a moment did I think of trying to catch up with her. Of leaving the Traverses in the lurch. With their car. And their cake. And me, even. They were expecting me.

I could no longer hide from myself the fact that Laure and I were now driving in opposite directions. I did not hope to hide it from myself, I only tried to present it to myself like this: that we each had a plan.

When I came to think about it, I actually had two. Firstly, going back to the Traverses. That was the clear one, the urgent one even. They must have been starting to worry. Then to go to Braz the next day. That would be my goal now. Arriving after a birthday party, on an island. Alone.

I was happy to have this goal, though. Cobbled together though it may be. If someone wants to feel sorry for me, I told myself, well, let them. I'm fine.

I just needed to sleep somewhere in the meantime. At the hotel, for example. Or maybe not. I was done with the hotel.

I was not too worried about the night, in fact. The night was just a detail. What I was actually thinking about was the next day. And Philippe, of course. But mostly me. The fact that I was going to Braz, that I would now definitely go there, the conditions under which I would go there, as well, but it was for Laure, too, I told myself, absolutely for her too, just not so soon, you see. Anyway, I'm not doing this out of altruism. But out of love. With all the limiting factors that that brings with it.

As for Philippe, he was not a problem either. I would arrive too late, that was all. Held up. The guy who came anyway. I would invent something, nothing much . . . a very heavy cold. No, not mine, I would say. Given that I've come. I'm only at the incubating stage.

Of course, Laure's plan was more vague. I could not attribute a more noble one to her than coming back to me. Calming down, in the first instance. Taking a step back, fine, but answering my calls, all the same. In the first instance, then, it did not appear that hard to me. Well, I liked the idea that we were sharing tasks between us, even if it was unequally. Gallantry, if you like. But sharing.

My hosts were not worried. In fact I came very close to thinking they had forgotten about me. Deliciously absentminded then, the Traverses, I thought.

"Did you have a problem?" Hélène asked, all the same.

"It was quite busy at the bakery. And I managed to get lost."

"Ah," said Gilles, "you must have gotten swept onto the D4. It carries right on beyond Bourgoin in a straight line, you can't see the turning. It used to happen to me, at first."

"That must be what it was," I said.

I was holding the cake in both hands. Hélène relieved me of it.

"By the way, have you reached a decision?" asked Gilles.

"Look," I said, "actually, yes, I'd like to accept your invitation, but it's really for the night. I feel embarrassed."

"No, you mustn't," protested Gilles, "you're sleeping here."

"And could you take me to the station in the morning?"

"Not too early," Gilles pointed out.

"Obviously," I said. "Thanks very much, anyway. And now, maybe I can help you."

"I think we've pretty much done everything," Hélène wanted to reassure me.

Gilles looked at his watch.

"We've got four hours to kill before the Neufincqs," he said.

I raised an eyebrow.

"They always arrive first," he explained. "Then Nicole. After that it varies. We often get Paul and Laetitia. Everyone's very nice, you'll see."

"I'm sure they are," I said.

"I'll show you around the house," he told me, "are you coming?"

I already knew their house, except for upstairs.

Gilles took my elbow. I would have really liked to know who he was. What he did for a living. And Hélène. And them. I had not seen them touch. Or meet each other's eyes. Mind you, if they had shown an interest in me, in something . . .

"What line of work are you in?" I asked him.

"Telephone canvassing in the textiles industry," he replied.

"What does that mean?"

He explained, briefly.

"I'd like to change jobs," he told me. "It's repetitive."

"Me too," I said.

"What do you do?"

"Nothing that's any more interesting," I said. "I don't love my work. I love my wife."

"Ah," he said.

"This paneling's nice," I said.

We were upstairs. Through a fanlight we could see out to the church. I craned on tiptoe: the square was empty, there was one car driving away on the right-hand side.

"Do you like it in the country?" I asked him.

"Yes," he said. "That's what's good about it."

"I think you're very welcoming," I said. "Both of you."

"Thank you."

I had nothing to say to him. I was bored, which was unhoped for: I had never seen boredom as a pastime. But, when things are not going too well, I now discovered, it works. Since being bored means constantly thinking there must be something better for you to do, but you cannot see it, do not have it, would like to have it. And I could see absolutely nothing else to do but to stay with the Traverses, to be with them for their party and spend the night at their house. Anyway.

I could have called Laure, of course. Once she was back home, for example. And even before. When I felt like it. If I wanted to know. And I did want to know.

Not right away.

Mentally I rubbed my hands. Gilles showed me the bedrooms.

The Traverses, who had no children, had friends. Friends whom they sometimes invited to stay, so these rooms had disparate furniture and made-up beds, twin beds in one and a double bed in the other, and rather dated wallpaper with obvious signs of paste here and there. Mind you, it was clean, and there were a few books lying on the chest of drawers in one of the rooms, and a pile of travel brochures and catalogues in a corner of the other. Which meant that in either of the rooms you could wait, busy yourself before going back down-stairs. I calculated that, if you arrived empty-handed and with no particular ideas in mind, you could last a couple of days there. That was far more than I needed, especially as I had not arrived empty-handed or with nothing on my mind. I had even brought a book, if I wanted.

I was shown around my hosts' bedroom and felt almost envious: light and airy, looking out over the surrounding land, and some trees in the distance with doves settling on them. The bed had a beautiful wickerwork headboard, there were warm drapes just to my taste, and wide wooden floorboards. And I felt I preferred the Traverses' bedroom to the people themselves, but I did not know what to make of that. There was no question that Gilles did not suit the decor. Hélène, I was not so sure, she would have had to come up, for me to see her there.

In fact, however little I liked the countryside, I could easily have been happy there.

In the meantime, my cold was asking for me again, wanting the physical expenditure it expected in terms of symptoms. This would invariably see me bent into a position that would solicit a mixture of compassion and awkwardness from Gilles, and leave me not exempt from a feeling of impotence. Gilles—inevitably embarrassed— suggested I should get some rest and lie down in one of the guest rooms.

I thanked him and refused the offer, but that did not take into account the fever. It was besieging me. I had not seen it coming and now it was there, making my insistence a mere stance. I could only mime standing upright, and it was not to attract pity that I brought my hand up to my forehead. With that too, I just wanted to know. I was hot.

"I'll find you some aspirin," Gilles said. "First on the right."

He had just pointed to the room with the twin beds, the smaller one. I was being pigeonholed. I am quite prepared to admit that I was alone. But still. I was the first. I had offered to help. And ill, too.

I criticized myself for this ill-feeling. Then absolved myself. Gilles and Hélène were annoying. I probably was too, but that was not the point. When you are tiresome, people cannot be bought with half measures. People overflow with thoughtfulness, I felt, but Gilles was not overflowing: he adapted to the demand. He came back up with two tablets.

"Here," he said.

He also gave me a glass of water. I thanked him and swallowed the tablets.

"I'll leave you on your own. You should get some sleep."

He slipped out, when, as far as I knew, he had nothing to do. I had to implement my sense of propriety: I really could not start hating him.

Someone was knocking. I had awakened quarter of an hour earlier, feverish, yes, in spite of the aspirin, but embraced by a familiar feeling. I could have been at home. Or perhaps have recently moved in. The Traverses were disappearing into a fog where the only thing I could really make out was their status as the owners.

I felt around my stomach to get an idea of my internal temperature. It was definitely me, incidentally. Me alone. They were the ones knocking. Him, at least. Gilles Traverse. Pushing the door open.

"Serge," he said.

I had forgotten about him too. As I emerged from my torpor he came back to me at the same time as I did myself. Like an item of clothing, I was getting dressed. I was aware of wanting to get up . . . not so much physically, though.

"How are you?" Gilles asked me.

He had popped his head through the doorway, as the doctor had that morning.

"Middling," I said.

Things were not at all good.

"The Neufincqs have just arrived," he told me. "I just wanted to let you know. You can stay in bed, of course."

"Thank you," I said.

Gilles pulled the door closed and disappeared. I could not really picture myself on my feet, but I had had enough of lying down. What I was really thinking about was the Neufincqs. I looked at my watch, they were on time. As anticipated. Now, I am usually on time myself, like the Neufincqs. There are very few of us, in fact. I did not want to miss them.

I felt like seeing these people who arrived on time, yes, that was it. To pick them like a flower as they arrived. It might also have been that I was anxious to be there, to be somewhere. I needed to establish some ascendancy. The idea that the Traverses occupied all the territory bothered me. I wanted to show myself a little. To live, maybe. I do not know.

I went down, relieved that the staircase was equipped

with a banister. I felt as if I were carrying my head, a task I undertook patiently, one hand pressed against the wall while I waited for my unsteady legs to come to my help, though they reacted too slowly to my muddled orders. Still, about halfway down my movements did become more or less coordinated, but it was less a reunification of my strengths than a federation of my weaknesses, producing what was basically a mediocre result: each stair seemed hopelessly deep and spongy, I came down them as if from the top of a sandy slope. It was only on the flat that the ground seemed, suddenly, to recover its firm consistency, and yet what it offered me in terms of support I interpreted more as resistance, rejection. I had to make headway with it, so to speak, in a conflictual way before considering it as what it became in the final few meters: an ally, when all was said and done, without which I would probably have ended up falling over.

I arrived in the living room when I was still at the stage of regrouping myself, my footsteps slow, although probably more or less serviceable, skirting around objects and even considering the surroundings and the people in it with the beginnings of acuity, if not interest, but not yet at the point when these capacities would be perceptible to anyone else, nor yet able to extract my consciousness completely from within myself. The Neufincqs were there, yes they were well and truly there, unbelievably present, standing facing me as if waiting for me at the end of a hospital corridor. Rather like visitors, I thought, the Traverses really should have told them what sort of state I was in. And, in fact, as I stepped forward to meet them, they watched me coming—not just the Neufincqs but the Traverses too, standing slightly in front of the Neufincqs so that they could introduce me to them, I told myself.

"Serge," Gilles did then say, indicating me to the woman who held out a hand to me.

"Christine," he said to me.

"Serge," Gilles repeated, this time for the benefit of the man who held out a hand to me.

"Jean-Marc," he said to me.

"Well, there we are," he added, addressing the Neufincqs. "Serge isn't feeling very well but he seems to have wanted to come down. Go back up whenever you feel like it, okay," he said to me before carrying on talking to them: "So then, Serge is just passing through, he'll be the only person who doesn't know anyone this evening. Would you like a drink, now?" he asked me.

"I'd love one," I said. "Alcohol can't be bad for me in my condition," I added, breaking into a smile for the Neufincqs: I felt I could see them more clearly than the Traverses who were confining themselves to a sort of background.

The Neufincqs then, one beside the other, inseparable, I told myself, and both of them punctual, having clearly arrived together, she having taken no more time than he had in her preparations, blond, short hair, sharp cheekbones, spindly fingers around the stem of the glass Hélène was handing to her. He was much taller than she was, jacketed and tied, looking more like a doctor than a visitor, in fact, his eye contact so strong it seemed to protrude, and I latched onto it like a foothold on a climbing wall, soothed at the thought that he would not let me go and, should the need arise, would even steady me with the odd amiable word.

"It was very good of you" (there he was, you see, not waiting a moment longer before speaking to me), "coming down in your state."

"Not at all," I said, thinking to myself that having come down I was now starting a steady climb and at the top, right up there, at the very summit of the tall Jean-

Marc Neufincq, the reward for my effort was in his grati-
fying expression, and in fact it gratified me in advance,
encouraging me along the way, now constructing an entire sentence to support me, and I realized that it was the
classic question about what I did for a living.

"Oh," I said, "you know, paper, phones, monitors.
Let's talk about you instead."

"Oh me," he said, "I run a little business. I'm in bathrooms, bathroom products. It's going pretty well but, to
be frank, what I really want to do is paint."

"He does paint, too," Christine Neufincq interrupted
with her spindly fingers and her oh-so soft expression.

"On Sundays," he said, "only on Sundays."

"Figurative?" I said.

"No," he told me, "not exactly." And so Jean-Marc
Neufincq told me about his painting, which I had difficulty imagining. I also had a glass in my hand now.

"Objects," Jean-Marc Neufincq was saying, "but
grafted, grafted onto each other, do you see what I mean?
So that—" he added, and then he paused.

While he tried to find the words he drank a mouth-
ful of kir. I had sat down in an armchair, with my legs
crossed, absolutely determined to listen to Jean-Marc

Neufincq talking to me about his painting, but also, when the opportunity arose, to give his wife Christine a chance to speak. I wanted the full complement of the Neufincqs and I eventually broke off from Jean-Marc to speak to his wife.

"And you?" I asked.

She did not do anything. They had four children. I was not sure what to say to her.

"Do you read?" I asked.

"Oh no!" she said. "Why? Why should I have to read?"

"True," I said. "I don't know. I don't read much either."

"But it's not that I don't read *much*," she protested, "I don't read *at all*."

I was just beginning to find her interesting, and I might well have explored the question more thoroughly were it not for the fact that, now that my glass was half empty, my head was beginning to spin.

"Anyway, you're punctual," I said. "I value punctuality."

Hélène and Gilles had just joined us, glass in hand, and I suspected they wanted to launch a new topic but, to my surprise, they said nothing. They smiled at the Neufincqs, apparently happy to see them again, but their smiles encompassed me, making a wide sweep, all in the same smile, so much so that I imagined that, in their eyes, I was like the Neufincqs, a guest, perhaps a potential friend, I told myself, unless they simply looked to us— the Neufincqs and myself—to be the ringleaders because they still had not said anything. I wondered exactly what was going on, perhaps nothing, but I had seen them more talkative. . . .

The Neufincqs and I now sat looking at each other.

"Well then," Jean-Marc Neufincq said to the Traverses, "how have you been since we last saw you? How long ago was it? When did we see each other? Do you remember, Christine?"

"It was in Blois, wasn't it?" Christine suggested.

"The weekend in Blois, yes," Jean-Marc Neufincq went on. "Just after Christmas, wasn't it? You couldn't find your shoes, do you remember?" he added, addressing Gilles. "We spent the whole of Sunday morning looking for them. It was incredible, that whole business with the shoes," he told me. "Do you remember where we found them?" he added, turning to both Traverses who,

I felt, did not seem to remember the anecdote with the shoes, at least not the principal figure concerned. Hélène, on the other hand, was trying to remember, then her face lit up.

"Oh yes," she said, and she put her hand on Gilles's arm, and he then started to remember. And the conversation took off: I grasped that the shoes had stayed in the trunk of the car on that Saturday, but I did not understand why or how Gilles had managed to walk into the hotel in his socks. I felt I was going through a difficult patch.

"Have you known each other long?" I interrupted them.

My question was addressed to the four of them then, and it was all four of them who replied, picking up where each other left off, mind you they were fortuitously arranged now, I had them all lined up, sweeping my eye over them . . . and for the first time I got the feeling I might be going too far, plowing on with a situation I could not control, particularly as my head was growing heavier and my nose was beginning to tickle, but I hung on or rather, having initiated the subject, I listened from somewhere in the depths of my exhaustion as they gave me their answers. Just hope I can hold out, I thought.

I do not know why I wanted to hold out. I could just as easily have gone back to bed and let them cope on their own with their reminiscing, especially as I knew that Laure might be back at home now, but at the same time I would have preferred it if she had been home for a while, had had time to settle down to something and then I would see, I thought to myself, she would have more to say to me. So I'm not missing out on anything by waiting. And I listened to the Traverses, and I listened to the Neufincqs: fifteen years already, fifteen years of friendship, almost a lifetime, I told myself, and I thought of mine, but I still could not remember anything. I tried to remember and all I could find—probably the association of ideas—was not me or Laure or anything, it was Serge, taking up residence in my vacant head, or nearly but in no great depth because I had not had news of Serge for a long time, a bit like me, in fact, I had not been getting much news about myself for a long time, except from Laure who had been passing news on to me up till now, keeping me informed about what I was, giving me useful indicators about how to move forward, one foot in front of the other, never farther than her, with her, always. And, even if Serge was a thousand kilometers away, at the moment he was the only one guiding me with the Traverses and the Neufincqs, it was not much really, and yet.

And yet nothing. Everything spooled on. I was no longer listening to the Traverses or the Neufincqs, sleep was threatening to catch up with me, I fought myself and the cold but I was going under, and it was unpleasant because Laure came and joined me again but we were no longer moving forward together, we were falling, sneezing together, separated by our fevers, each in our own beds projected into a vacuum while thermometers rained down around us, then there were hailstones of tablets. I pressed a button above my head to call the nurse, and I saw Gilles Traverse get to his feet.

"Ah," he said, "that must be Nicole."

I got to my feet, though you could not say I had really been asleep. We got to our feet, the Neufincqs, Hélène, and myself, watching Gilles open the door down the hall.

"Nicole!" he cried. And I realized that everything was happening just the way it should, in the correct order, Nicole after the Neufincqs, fine, Gilles greeting the new arrival effusively, as if she might not have come, or might not have come in time, congratulating himself for this miracle—hypocritically, I told myself, unless he was just being very stupid, or perhaps simply friendly. It did not matter much to me. In fact, it suited me just fine that Nicole should be there now, that the party should be panning out so predictably, especially as I had my own part to play in it, and I was in fact moving over toward Nicole, not in the same way as the Neufincqs and Hélène because—in my case—the floorboards seemed to be swimming beneath my feet, but probably in the same spirit as them, just waiting until it was my turn to greet the new guest.

There were kisses, although it struck me the Neufincqs had not known Nicole as long as the Traverses, if you went by the slight reserve they displayed. In fact, I preferred that because when I came to shaking Nicole's hand after the Neufincqs you could say that, with me, she was sort of coming down a notch in familiarity. Yes, but just one notch; actually, it was not really a question of status. Perhaps also because, apart from the fact that I was there before Nicole, it must have seemed to her that the Neufincqs and the Traverses knew me quite well, given that Gilles was introducing me with one hand on my shoulder, pushing me gently toward his friend, and the Neufincqs were smiling as they watched as if this were a rather solemn, touching announcement, like an enthronement, like this great guy has just joined us, his name is Serge, let us welcome him and thank the Lord, but let us not forget to pray for his recovery, because, standing there facing Nicole, my cold was flaying me again and I now had only one hand with which to stifle the spasm I could feel rising.

"Pleased to meet you," I did manage to say. "Excuse me."

And I turned away from Nicole, masking my nose with my hand, but I had had time to glimpse her, vaguely. She was a young woman whose cheerfulness was already registered in a smile that seemed to result less from a movement of her lips than from an indigenous stretching action—a gentle one, probably, but one from which she had no means of regressing so that you could not help being curious to know how, in muscular terms, she would express sadness. But what really struck me was that she was carrying a guitar in her hand, an acoustic one judging by its appearance, in a case, but a guitar all the same, I told myself. She's come to sing, I thought, don't let's forget this is a party, there *are* people who don't balk at the idea of humming a little tune on such occasions, don't pretend you didn't know that, you are perfectly well aware of that, always have been, not to mention that with birthdays you invariably sing, when the time comes for the cake, you know that too, and you never manage to do it, to sing, you know that as well, that when it comes to the cake and the little song you clam up, not one sound passes your lips but you do actually do the moves, mutely miming that consensual braying with its unbearable and inane empathy, and smiling even, going so far as to smile, but only with your eyes, given that your lips are unavailable, totally given over to their feeble work of imitation. Still, I told myself, that's not right away, save your strength till the time comes, nothing's really started. In fact, at the moment they're just waiting for everyone else and getting Nicole a drink.

There were now six of us, then, sitting around the little table in the living room, and I wondered whether, as the numbers rose, I felt less and less alone or whether, conversely, I was beginning to get that feeling you get in the middle of a crowd, that characteristic isolation exacerbated by the mass, and, to be honest, I did not have a clue, I felt as if I no longer knew anything much. And perhaps, also, I was no longer trying to know. The wine, probably, which was being poured into my glass again; the cold, of course, which meant I saw Nicole as a guitar player, a woman reduced to her instrument, in fact, even though she had left it in the hall in favor of a glass so that she now seemed to be missing something and her indigenous smile struck me as being even more fixed, almost deceitful, denying this sort of amputation I was attributing to her, the absence of her guitar being like the absence of a limb, and I thought at one point I caught her casting furtive, agonized glances in its direction, from where she was sitting. But perhaps that was a projection on my part, fueled by my fear that she might want to use it even at this aperitif stage, when we were still getting our bearings (weren't we?), particularly me, and it seemed to me that someone was telling Nicole about me at the time, and her gaze floated over the surface of me as if I were a rather badly focused photograph and the person was explaining the caption to her because it was not sufficiently detailed in its original form.

In any event, we did not stay alone very long, if I can put it like that. We had reached that stage in the evening when things speed up: people arrive, of course, and they arrive more and more quickly, in groups sometimes, so that there were now twelve of us around the little table, some standing, in fact, and among them there were two couples, hands clamped around their glasses poised at the end of arms bent at right angles, while a pile of clothes was beginning to form on a bench in the hall, and the bell rang every five minutes. Gilles was only introducing me to half of them now, too much to do. Either way, I had given up getting out of my chair, I do not think I would have managed it.

There was a moment, which I felt stood out more than others, when we sat down for dinner. I had to get up, of course, but not for very long, I seem to remember I was one of the very first to be seated, not the first, though. I seem to think Gilles showed me to a chair. So I was soon sitting facing people I had only just met, Paul and Laetitia, probably, each flanked by a member of the opposite sex, fairly disparate characters, including a man who looked very tall sitting down. In any case, Hélène brought in the first course and Gilles poured the wine.

"Everyone's here now, except for Karine," he muttered to himself as he moved about the room—mind you, we were already very cramped. What is more, I was sitting next to a charming, smiley, simple woman (Denise, perhaps), who presented only one inconvenience in that she was left-handed, so that our elbows knocked when we lifted our forks, and I had to shift myself slightly toward a man who was no such nuisance, considerably older than me, I think, and he hardly seemed to speak or move, feeding himself slowly in erratic mouthfuls, as if thinking about something completely different, or perhaps he had simply eaten before coming out. I was not very hungry either, and the fever was making me hot, so were the people, and the wine, I had very little room to move or to think. Mind you, I was not thinking, a bit about Laure, perhaps, knowing that she would be home now, and I would probably have liked to call her, I would even have liked her to be there, I would definitely have told her to come, in fact—I did not feel I had the strength to join her. Of course there was no question of joining her or of suggesting she should come, incidentally, I am just saying what I was thinking, and my thoughts were far from anchored in concrete facts at that stage, I could no longer visualize the situation very well, I could easily have got up from the table and said I was leaving—the idea did drift over me, to be honest, as everything else did. At the same time, it was quite out of the question for me to move, I knew I would not leave the Traverses until the following morning, I would just have liked it if, some time in the next hour, someone had helped me get to bed. I was starting to yawn and was even beginning to embrace the idea of resting my head on the shoulder next to me, given that it belonged to a man with the advantageous qualities of being absolutely silent and steady . . . he might not even notice.

All the same, I was eating. There was a succession of different dishes. It was good, I think, I am almost sure it was good, I could hear people congratulating Hélène. On top of this, there were three conversations going on, and from time to time I lent each of them an ear, particularly the one which, I eventually grasped, was about me, less in relation to my general status than my state of health, of course, a conversation that my posture alone could fuel, without recourse to words, and I settled for nodding my head in acquiescence, smiling occasionally. It was quite easy, in fact, and from time to time I would venture a "How about you?" after which I would hear less a reply than an echo, a sort of modulation of my question that did nothing to move the conversation forward, just a collection of sounds, a hubbub of voices that I could re-ignite rather like a deaf man who has not come to terms with his condition—smiling, for your information. To be honest, I was no longer in control of anything, but still people seemed to like me, no danger of a lynching, I noted, even though I was laying it on a bit, I did know that, but, I should point out, I had not chosen to be ill.

I had not chosen anything, in fact. Nothing at all. I was there by chance, if you want to call it chance that sometimes propels our lives when they run away with us, in which case chance would be, at worst, a sort of letting go—I am prepared to admit that I was letting myself go a bit, yes, but I fail to see how I could have taken any initiative in the situation, particularly as no one was expecting anything of me and, to be honest, I did not need anything either, except from Laure, who was not really there to worry about and whom I was not going to call right away, that much was sure, I was not going to interrupt the conversation that Denise had the goodness to embark on with me, asking whether I had known the Traverses long.

"Since this morning," I said. "Gilles picked me up hitchhiking. How about you?" I added, now well broken in to such mundane exchanges.

"Oh, me," she said.

They all said "oh, me" at that party when you asked them "How about you?"; I was dealing with modest people, and that was no bad thing. Incidentally, Denise went on to talk about herself right away, particularly—thanks to a knocking of our elbows—about how clumsy she was. It was embarrassing actually, or at least it would have become embarrassing if I had listened to her as attentively as she was hoping, but that is not what I did at all, I started telling her about Laure, and she seemed to be interested, she seemed to come out of herself, but not me, oh no, and I noticed that the motionless gentleman on my left was listening in: I felt happier not saying any more.

The dessert arrived, I was going to say by chance but it was at that precise moment, at the precise moment when all the lights suddenly went out that Hélène brought the cake. And, however few people I may have known that evening, I certainly knew the cake well . . . and what exactly does that mean, I asked myself, to know the cake better than the people at a party? But I did not have time to ponder the question because it was at that point that Nicole, who must have left the table at the same time as Hélène without my noticing, reappeared, accompanying Hélène but also accompanying herself on the guitar, striking up that dreaded, terrifying tune while Hélène held the cake aloft, with her arms at chest height, her smiling face ghostly in the candlelight, which flickered of course, and all around me people opened their throats in song, even the shy Denise beside me came out of her shell, deafening me, and even the motionless gentleman on my left, but I myself did not move a muscle, I did not even pretend, I settled for taking out my hankie, keeping one eye on the proceedings. No one was interested in me, anyway.

I made the most of this to get away. As everyone had gotten to their feet, yelling and then clapping while Gilles leaned forward and—once he was over the surprise of discovering his own portrait on top of the cake—forcefully blew out the candles, then made a witty comment about this exploit, I too had stood up. I am not really sure how, but I had well and truly stood up, anyway, and, pushing off from the back of my chair to give myself a bit of impetus, I set off amid a general movement that ensued as everyone dispersed toward their bags to get Gilles's presents, but I was actually heading for the living room where I had noticed a cordless phone resting on its base unit. I dialed our number in Paris and, I am not really sure whether I was expecting this or not, more likely not, I think, Laure picked up.

There was a pause that corresponded less to my distracted state—although that was genuine enough, incidentally—than to my rather belated realization that Laure, back home listening to the earpiece, would have been able to hear a hubbub in the background that could only have sounded to her like a party, one particular party—Philippe's, on the island of Braz.

"It's me," I said eventually. "Are you home?"

"Yes," she said. "How about you?"

Funny hearing that coming from someone I actually knew when those words had punctuated the whole evening, but it was not reassuring, I did not dare lie to her by saying that I had arrived in Braz, but at the same time I could not see what else to tell her, I did not feel like launching into explanations she would not really understand, or into any kind of explanation for that matter. In fact, I did not feel like explaining myself, I did not want to lie either, though: she deserved better than being lied to. Still, I did lie.

"I'm there," I said.

"I can hear," she said. "How's it going?"

I did not want her asking me that kind of question either, I was the one with the questions, far more crucial ones.

"It's going very well," I said. "Do you want to speak to Philippe?" I added, perhaps because of the wine, or the fever, I did not really care anyway, she could easily have said yes and I would have said no, you can't speak to

Philippe, I'm not there, at Philippe's place, I'm at Gilles's birthday party this evening, which is good enough, isn't it? But she did not want to speak to Philippe, she did not want anything, that is what she was now telling me, I was getting used to it but I still did not like it, I would have liked a woman who wanted something, anything, something that *I* could give her preferably, but not her.

"If you only wanted something I couldn't give you," I said, "that would help, that would be something at least."

"It's not that," she said.

"Well, what is it then?" I asked.

"I've forgotten what you said before your question," she said. I felt caught out then, I could not remember the thread of my thoughts, or what I had said before the question, or the question. I think I was starting to feel slightly dizzy.

"Listen," I said, and I suddenly wanted to cry. I did not even hear her answer, but I could no longer remember whether I had asked her anything.

"What did you say?" I said. "Hello?"

"I'm going to hang up," she said. "It would be better."

"No, it wouldn't be better," I heard myself shout and that was when I realized that Nicole, who had put down her guitar, was watching me sternly, or perhaps anxiously, whereas Denise looked decidedly anxious, and she was not the only one, in fact, they were all watching me, with the presents scattered over the table, Gilles himself had stopped dead halfway through untying a gift-wrap bow.

"Don't hang up," I said gently. "Wait a minute, I'll explain." And I looked at them all, looking at me, but she had hung up and I went on looking at them. I wanted her to be there and to slap her, but it was all of them I was looking at.

"I'm so sorry," I said, and it was Gilles who, abandoning his parcel, came over to me, kindly, and suggested I should go back to the table.

They sat me back down. I did not say anything, I did not know what to say, I looked at the presents, alone, sitting among all those people standing up, thinking for a moment that it was for me, all this, the knickknacks, books, CDs, gadgets, photos, and radios that Gilles was unwrapping almost unwillingly, because he had to, perhaps hesitating because I was there, maybe even thinking he could surrender one of his presents for my benefit, that idea must have been just flitting through his head

by chance when a sort of inverted version of the same idea
was flitting through mine, too.

"Excuse me," I said, and I stood up. No one stopped
me, they were all amazed that I could actually manage it,
and I could feel them looking at me again as I undertook
the difficult journey toward the front door where I found
my bag, and I knelt and rummaged through it, revealing
sweaters, my toilet bag, a pair of sneakers, and then at last
what I was looking for, the package I had made sure I
took when I left Laure. I headed back toward the table
now, carrying it with two hands like some oblation in its
slightly crumpled wrapping paper, then handed it to
Gilles and wished him a happy birthday.

First there was Gilles's surprise, then clapping that I reckoned was at least partly intended for me: I was clearly back
in play at that point, but I was not totally capable of enjoying the fact. I hated Laure and I watched Gilles who
was pausing before opening my present, which was quite
a lot to take in in just a few seconds, but first I was thinking about the present, of course—it is strange how in
certain situations the behavior of people who are actually
there can require so much energy when it is the ones who
are not there who are keeping your heart busy and steadily
ravaging it. But that was how it was, it bothered me that
Gilles, who still looked surprised, should be so doubtful,
hesitating to open my present before those the others had
already put on the table.

So then Gilles kept his eye on me as he put my parcel to one side and carried on with his unwrapping, and I

was afraid that—logically—he would not come to my present until the very end, which would have been another way of making me the center of attention, I suppose, but he really had no way to avoid this, and neither did I: he just had to deal with that present now that it was there. In fact we were all conscious of this, to varying degrees, most of us unaware that I had not physically had the time to effect this purchase since arriving at the Traverses' house, others—like Gilles himself and Hélène, and perhaps to a lesser degree the Neufincqs—piecing together the only possible explanation, that I had made use of my errand to the bakery to go somewhere else, in heaven knows which improbable little shop, and find something to give to my host, justifying the delay, as they knew, by citing the line at the bakery but also the fact that I had got lost, nothing about my stopping by at the hotel, of course, that was my life, wasn't it, that had nothing to do with them, because Laure was not the only one I was lying to, I was lying to everyone, and it was not over yet, they did not know what I was going to tell Philippe the next day.

That's just the way it is, I told myself. I don't know why, I still don't know why I've come to this, to lying now, but that's the way it is. And Gilles carried on unwrapping, it was coming to the end, now, they had pretty much gone into raptures about everything, the tie, the razor . . . and that was when the doorbell rang.

"It's Karine," said Gilles. "She's the only person who would come after dinner."

Hélène went to open the door, and it was Karine, apologetic, dark-haired, coming in, taking off her jacket, "I'm so sorry, Gilles," a bag in her hand, bright-eyed, interesting legs exposed at the bottom of a pencil skirt. "Happy birthday. I see I'm in time for the cake at least."

We were all standing around the table at that point, except for me, I was still sitting. Gilles obviously opened Karine's parcel, saw the contents, made his exclamation, kissed her. All that was left now was my present: he opened it. It was right out of my hands now, I knew nothing about Gilles's taste.

"Oh!" he said. "Incredible!" he exclaimed excitedly against all expectations. "Can you believe this, Hélène? It only gave out last week. Where did you find this?" he asked me, brandishing my present like a silver goblet, but he realized that for most of the people there the question was incongruous.

"It doesn't matter," he went on, "it's really kind of you and it couldn't be better timing. We'll use it right away tomorrow morning," he concluded, putting my present down on the table.

"How about cutting this cake now, then?"

Hélène set to work, slicing up the portrait of Gilles, being particularly careful to spare the eyes. I personally received a corner of his mouth, Nicole a cheek, and so on, and soon all that was left of our scattered host was the original who invited all of us back into the living room for coffee. There was a general move, then, once again, not as synchronized as before, probably weighed down by the meal, so that our regrouping in the living room was a staggered process with some elements openly staying behind, creating little pockets of resistance, carrying on with conversations that were now strengthened by their temporary isolation, forearmed against the dispersing effect that their involvement in the jumble of the party would inevitably bring about.

I just followed, falling in step—to use that military image—with Gilles in whose eyes I had scored a few points in advance, in advance of what, I asked myself, I'm not sure I've got much else to ask of him. For the time being, though, he was useful to me, or his shoulder was at least as I leaned on it in a friendly sort of way when, to be honest, I needed it for support. And so we all ended in the living room, and I was put on a long sofa, next to the arm.

I looked at the people opposite me, more or less in a circle, some on chairs, and I discovered two or three faces I had not registered around the table, including that of a rather heavy woman with red cheeks who, I realized, had come in an apron, unless her dress imitated or rather integrated such an accessory by creating an impression, an impression made by the dress, then, or my own impression, perhaps, which was trying to convince me that this woman had not been employed in the kitchen, and—in the state I was in, which was very obviously feverish—I could not work out whether the correct impression was the first one, the one given by the dress, I really could not make it out and I would almost have gotten up to go and check if I had had the strength to, but no, instead I made a choice that this woman might have interpreted badly, if she had been worrying about it: I stopped looking at her, I lost interest in her even though she could have been interesting. I am not judging her by saying that, she was just a woman I knew absolutely nothing about, that was all.

I focused my attention on Nicole again. I preferred keeping myself busy looking at people, in the hope that it would help me get over my fury, by which I mean Laure. I forced myself to forget as much as possible, for now, and I turned back to Nicole because of her guitar, hoping to distract myself with the fear—and I tried to fuel this fear so that it overtook me completely—that the aforementioned Nicole would pick up the aforementioned guitar that had been left in the hall probably, although perhaps not put away in its case, and so I sat there waiting for her to go and get it. But that is not what happened at all, time passed and Nicole did not go and get her guitar, and I started to think—and this idea became clearer as the evening went on—that she had brought it with the sole purpose of accompanying *Happy birthday to you*, with that sole purpose and no other, either because she only knew the chords for that tune, or because she did not like playing the instrument any more than that, or because no one in the present company really appreciated her style and she knew that and did not want to impose her playing at all costs, or because in everyone's perception this was essentially a party without music, but none of these reasons satisfied me, which had the fortuitous effect of keeping me busy thinking.

So, as I said, time passed, and there I was, at one point half fascinated by the cook with the unnecessary apron, then by Nicole and my obsession with her guitar that she never strummed again, and now lulled—although with occasional twitches and starts—by a conversation that was drawing in the majority of guests and that was about the war we were not fighting, us, the French . . . an allusion to my nationality that shocked me, actually, especially there and then when I would have liked to outline my contours more clearly, to draw them tighter, basically, and not extend them to what struck me as a rather large entity in which I seemed to bob about. At one point I was even afraid someone was going to ask my opinion, but no, they respected me, I think, giving me the sort of looks you give to a potential ally, as opposed to a secure one, while—rather than actually *nodding* my head—I wobbled it from side to side. Besides, the conversation broke up, and now there were several distinct groups again, or groups that I could more or less make out, and I tried to watch their various members: those I knew, those I did not know so well, those I did not know at all, yet, at that stage in the evening, a couple of them, no more, including a woman I had not really seen, as she was sitting next to me on the sofa and had launched into a conversation with me about my condition, yet again, it was as good a subject as any other, after all, and I latched onto it half-heartedly, catching sight of the Neufincqs and the Traverses opposite me (the old guard, you could say) involved in their own animated conversation. But I no longer thought of them as people I knew better than the others, they were blending in, into the others: there were just people, faces and noise in front of me, and I was nowhere and with no one, there was only Laure in the distance and this voice near me drifting away, then coming back, trundling out its slurred words that I could not always make out and to which I replied without even realizing it, because you have to reply, you cannot shut yourself away in silence like that, no, so I replied, not initiating anything, but replying, and that voice—not even the mouth that I could not see, or hardly, which I was not trying to see, anyway, I did not have the strength—that voice grew familiar to me, as the Traverses had that morning. Not that I knew the woman uttering it, but what it said, yes, the subject, then, not my cold, no, but, after a while, a word I must have dropped inadvertently and that was now coming back to me, a place name, to be precise, and I woke up a little then.

"Excuse me?" I said.

And the voice replied, "Braz, yes, I'm heading to the island of Braz tomorrow, too. If you like I could take you there. You don't have a car, right?"

Of course I was looking at her now, it was the least I could do. And I really saw her, her eyes, her mouth, her blouse, but no more. I had enough with her face and her torso, I wanted to see the face and the torso—that struck me as enough but indispensable, absolutely indispensable —of this woman who was going to Braz the following day. And I almost asked her whether she knew Philippe, whether she was going to Philippe's house. In which case, I considered, there would have been two of us there that evening who would be celebrating two birthdays on consecutive days, and one of them with the same delay, exactly the same. And so, with the freedom granted by the general wavering condition to which I was prey, all I actually asked her was why she was going to Braz.

"How about you?" she said.

I would have preferred it if she had answered first. But it was my duty to remain polite and, as there was no question of my telling her the truth about the two birthdays, their succession being, in my case, very real; as I refused to pass myself off as a birthday maniac, and, what is more, one who was not even capable of nurturing his mania by proving himself punctual for both events; as I did not, so to speak, want to appear to be a failed maniac, I told her I was going to see a friend who had a house there. Which was in fact the truth and which now allowed me to return her "How about you?", although I was afraid that, in the hazy discussion that had preceded her rejoinder about Braz, I might already have told her my life story. But it was too late anyway. Besides, I could not care less. I had started lying that evening, and my dignity did not pose me any particular problems.

She had friends in Braz too, then. She was going to stay with them for a week. She was actually trying to find somewhere to buy, like them.

"Like a lot of people," she elaborated. "It's becoming harder and harder to find anything, and it's very expensive. Still, it's a decision I've made. No cars," she said, "two restaurants, beaches everywhere, the only sounds are the seagulls and the clicking of changing gears on bicycles . . ."

"You know it better than I do," I said. "I've never been there," I explained.

"In fact, I might know this Philippe," she went on.

I did not remember naming him. But, as I did not remember the rest either, I was not overly surprised.

"Braz, it's very small," she said. "What does your friend look like?"

"Well," I replied, and as I described Philippe for her—to the best of my abilities—I was actually looking at her, but not just her, a face with some sharp angles, then, but in proportion, like Hélène's, I thought, because I was also looking at Hélène who was watching us now, not so angular (but in proportion too) as this woman, as if she were an earlier version, not so pronounced, Hélène I mean, Hélène to whom I addressed a smile, along with the Neufincqs. No, no, I smiled at them too—the Neufincqs—I haven't forgotten you, dear friends, but this is inclined to happen at parties, you get talking, you find areas of interest, and inevitably gravitate around them. Thanks for everything, I seemed to be saying to them, or so I imagined, because they were pretending they had lost interest in me now, turning to their own conversation, clutching in their hands newly arrived little glasses that were still empty, and, having been passed down a long chain, two of them ended up with this woman and myself.

"No alcohol, thank you," she said.

"Yes please," I said.

"I think I might know who you mean," she said. "Everyone pretty much knows everyone else over there."

"And do Gilles and Hélène know Braz?" I asked, holding my glass beneath the mouth of a bottle, suddenly noticing that it was Gilles who was pouring it out. Never mind, I thought, but I did actually wait until he had filled my glass and moved away before carrying on.

"Do Gilles and Hélène not go there?" I went on. "Have you ever talked to them about the island?"

"But I don't really know Gilles and Hélène very well, you know. I hardly know anyone here, I'm here because of Paul."

"Do you know Paul?" I asked. "Paul as in Paul and Laetitia?"

"Yes," she said. "There, to your left. Do you know them, then?" she asked me.

"No," I replied. "Of course I don't know them. I'm like you, I don't know anyone here, I just caught their names in passing, I'm just passing myself, I must have told you that."

"You haven't told me much," she said. "What you've mostly done is blow your nose."

"I'm sorry," I said.

"Please don't be," she said. "It doesn't bother me, I've had my flu jab. You must have a temperature, haven't you?"

"Yes," I said. "But haven't we already talked about this? At the beginning?"

"Yes," she said, "but you didn't seem to be listening to me, so I'm asking you again now if you've got a temperature, and you've told me you have, so we could start again from there, couldn't we?"

"Yes, I guess," I said. "If you like, but it's not a very exciting subject," and my feverish eyes met hers.

"Let's forget about my temperature for a bit," I suggested. "Let's talk about you instead. There's a chance it'll be more interesting, isn't there? You must be more interesting than my temperature. Because otherwise . . ." I added, although I did not want to ruffle her, except I already had, which did not stop her from replying "oh," but she did not add the "me."

"Oh, I don't know," she replied, then, as if I had not said anything upsetting, "I'm feeling fine, I'm heading for Braz tomorrow, and then I go and meet you and it makes a change, you see, I find you reasonably pleasant and that makes a change, yes, I only know nice sporty people. Do you do any sport?" she asked.

"No," I said, "none at all. I don't think I can remember developing a single muscle, but," I added, for what it was worth and encouraged by her open-mindedness, "I'm not trying to please you, I don't give a damn. About pleasing you, I mean. That's the least of my worries, you know."

"I know," she said. "I've noticed. It doesn't bother me either. Mind you, even if this may be a pain, I like people like you," she added.

Good god, I thought, what do I have to do to stop this woman liking me, insult her, turn my back on her, tell her I don't like her . . .

"I like people like you," she was saying, then, "not sporty, not friendly, not talkative, and even with a temperature, yes," she confirmed, "at least you have something to say for yourself, not like them, what do they have to say for themselves, hey? Can you tell me that?"

"But they're very kind," I protested. "They're good people."

"They're not good people at all," she said. "And, anyway, I don't know what the hell I'm doing here, I hardly know Gilles, I should never have come to this party when I'm leaving so early in the morning, I'm going to go home, I'll wait a bit then I'll go home. How shall we leave it for tomorrow, you and me? Do you still want me to take you?"

I did not remember ever having wanted her to, to take me, so I now asked myself for the first time how I should reply, knowing by deduction that this was the second time she had offered—to take me, I mean—and I told myself that I was going to say yes anyway, that it would mean arriving in Braz earlier, and I wanted to get Braz over and done with, and Philippe too, and only then would I see about Laure, by going home, except that I could see earlier, by calling her back, but in the meantime I was going there, to Braz, given that Laure had not asked me to come back, she hadn't asked me anything like that, had she? No.

"No what?" replied the woman next to me, who seemed to be reading my thoughts to the extent that she grasped those that escaped my lips.

"No nothing," I said. "Well, yes, actually, I'd like it if you could take me. I really have to get to Braz tomorrow so the quicker the better," careful, I'm not going to tell her everything out loud, I stalled myself. "Thank you."

"Right," she said.

Right, I said to myself. Now that I know what I'm doing tomorrow and how I'm going to do it, what's going on here? Am I going back to sleep?

"I hope I haven't shocked you," she said.

"Excuse me?" I said.

"I was just saying I hope I haven't shocked you," she said, apparently for the second time, "suggesting you should stay at my house tonight, given that I live alone, but I'm leaving early tomorrow and I don't want to disturb Gilles and Hélène by coming to pick you up from their house at dawn."

"Um," I said, "I don't know. I need to make a phone call."

"You can make as many phone calls as you like," she said. "That's nothing to do with it. Do you at least understand what I'm saying? Are you listening? Are you feeling terrible?"

"Not too good, anyway," I said. "Your house," I said. "Yes. To sleep, is that it?"

"Pretty much," she said.

"Well then, why not," I said, and I wondered whether I really wanted to leave the Traverses right away this evening, I think not but, on the other hand, going somewhere this evening seemed better, it was like a guarantee that I would go somewhere the next day, given that. Just, I was only wondering whether I was actually capable of it. Physically.

"Are you going to ask me to drive?" I asked. "Tomorrow."

"Don't worry about that."

"Then, I'd be very happy to spend the night at your house," I said. "But I have to make a call."

"I gathered that," she said. "Make your call now, then."

"I'd rather wait."

"You're intriguing," she said. "What's this about?"

"Aha," I said. "It's a long story. No joke at all. I couldn't even tell you if I wanted to."

"You don't want to."

"No."

People were watching us now. And I realized that we were talking across their silence. They were all there, the Traverses, the Neufincqs, Paul and Laetitia, Nicole, Karine, Denise, the cook, the motionless man and the others, pointedly silent, probably initially because of lulls in their conversations, awkward pauses we had not noticed, but now they were attentive—albeit discreetly —as if, with nothing better to do, we (this woman and I) had become the focus of their interest. But when they realized I had noticed, they picked up where they had left off as best they could, lamely reigniting their conversations with self-conscious expressions that upset me. I hated myself for making them feel uncomfortable. What I originally wanted was for the party to run its course and for me to be granted only the necessary degree of attention, no more. Now I had become an embarrassment again, and that is probably what made my mind up, not that I was far off from a decision anyway, I was already in Braz by then, almost. I whispered to the woman that we could go whenever she wanted, now, that I did not want to hold her up. I just had to say good-bye and thank you properly.

"Okay," she said. "Me too. I suppose I'm going to get up first."

"That would be good," I said.

I tried, as she got up and I was still sitting down, to see what she looked like on her feet, this woman who was taking me to Braz the next day in her car, having offered to put me up for the night in order, she had said, not to disturb anyone. And I mean it when I say I tried because, in the state I was in, the low angle to which I was constrained produced a distortion, stretching her upward and accentuating her facial angles, making her, I told myself, harsher than she probably was, less pleasing, although she was undeniably attractive. In any case, this was not an ugly woman so, I thought, no one here will be surprised, or not extremely, that we should be leaving this gathering, the two of us, in step with each other . . . together, in other words, if we are going to be realistic about this. We are not mismatched: this woman may be attractive, yes, but I for my part am hardly blighted by any deformity, even though I was blighted, but not deformed. I'm presentable, I told myself, just dying of a cold, that's all, so what? There's also our agreement, between this woman and myself, our affinities—in everyone else's eyes, I mean, between ourselves it's quite different, that's none of their business, and what does it matter if they think the two of us are going to fall into each other's arms the minute we get through the door, in a pinch you could say they were accessories to it, they'll think the party achieved something.

I found it helped, seeing this from their position. It helped me move from mine, not that anything had happened in that direction yet. I loved being on that sofa, it had a tall enough back to lean my head on, not to mention the armrest. Besides, I was having trouble getting used to the idea of abandoning the Traverses right away. It was as if I had been using them, from the start, like one of my hankies, and I was now throwing them away, although I was leaving them with my present, a sort of compensation that encouraged me to heave myself up, very gently, pushing off with the palms of my hands. They were no longer looking at me, anyway; at that point they were probably thinking that I had huddled deeper into the sofa after the verbal effort I had produced in talking to this woman who was now saying good-bye to them, not that they could see any clear link, at that point, with my departure that was now imminent because I had actually gotten to my feet.

And, now vertical, I managed to stay standing. I suddenly saw everything from above, the people, yes, but also myself, on my feet, ready to leave with this woman. She had materialized at a good time, in fact, everything was turning out for the best, I could just go with the flow, cursing Laure and wondering what she was brewing back home, where it was logical she should now be, in a sense, but not without me, was it? I did not really like the fact that she had induced me to distance myself from her as if, basically, I had chosen not to go home. And the fact that I was setting off again did not militate in her favor, because, with every step I took to get closer to her (even though, in geographical terms, I was getting farther away from her), she was the one drawing away without even moving a muscle.

Standing, then, and probably ready to leave, but she had it coming to her, time and space were playing into my hands. I expanded them, time and space, I drew them out and, even if I was afraid the thread would snap under the pressure, I was actually the one holding her, with the help of the others, too. Because I can obviously not claim that I would have managed it on my own. With help from the Traverses and all the others, yes. With this woman, too, who was unexpected, unforeseen, and who was clearly taking an interest in me, which suited me very well just so long as she did not entertain the hope that it was reciprocal. I just wanted her to understand that I accepted her and that even her putting me up, later, did not bother me. I felt as if I knew her, too. In fact it was not impossible that I had, at some time in the past, left a woman like her.

In the meantime, I went and joined her. To be precise, I made a wide detour toward the Traverses. They looked dismayed. I think they had spotted my maneuver.

"You get along well with Florence," said Gilles, extending his hand with a thin smile. "Are you leaving with her?"

"It's not what you're thinking," I said. "It turns out that Florence—and actually you've just told me what her name is—is going to Braz tomorrow. Did you know that? And she's giving me a lift there. Do you know Braz?"

"No," replied Gilles, "not at all. But that's great for you! That's great!" he repeated, raising his voice in the hopes of finding someone to join the conversation, someone who really could have appreciated how lucky I was, because I was apparently not best placed to do so, in his opinion. But he was not only enthusiastic, he was also disappointed and, even though he was exclaiming so loudly in the hopes of finding a witness, I sensed—beneath the cheery exterior—a sort of lamentation.

"I don't know Braz or Florence, except by name," he told me. "Both of them. It's Paul who invited her."

"So, are you leaving?" Hélène cut in, having just joined us and holding out her hand to me now. "Well, good-bye Serge. I've enjoyed meeting you."

"Me too," I said.

What I had trouble putting across was that I was being sincere.

"It's an opportunity," I said, "you understand. And she would never have picked me up hitchhiking."

"It all depends," Gilles pointed out, as if the atmosphere were relaxing (but I would have been surprised). "You never know."

"I would have taken the train, anyway," I said.

"Oh," said Hélène.

Florence was coming over toward us. She had just said good-bye to Paul and Laetitia, and a few others.

"I'm going to have to leave," she said. "I have to get up early."

I bowed my head.

"I'm going away," explained Florence.

This was unbearable. I looked back up, looked the Traverses squarely in the eye.

"Right," said Florence. "Thank you for a lovely party."

I nodded. Florence was not looking at me. Maybe she's actually ashamed of me, I thought. She may be ashamed of me but she's taking me anyway. She's attracted to me sexually. Her problem is she has no self-control. She's attracted to men who are ill—fine. Not something you can admit to all and sundry.

If I had not been with her I would have liked my hosts to have seen me to the door. This was different, though. We were sort of abandoning them, I felt. And, as Florence had told them we were leaving and as she only seemed to be talkative with me, we *were* leaving. We started to turn away, the two of us. But, when it came down to it, I could not get used to the idea that the Traverses were not seeing us out. I turned discreetly to see whether they were actually following us and—in the event that that was not the case—I was prepared to dress up my glance with a little wave. Still, I never found out whether they were going to follow us or whether they at least felt some regret not to be because, at that very moment, I tripped on a kilim that had rucked in several places with the to and fro of the party. I lurched forward, just managing to grab hold of Florence's arm but she, unfortunately, was unable to stop my fall. I dragged her to the ground with me, and we landed messily, me fractionally before her as I let go of her to protect my face, not altogether succeeding in stopping my nose coming into contact with the floor or my left knee from knocking it with relative violence, tempered though it was by the indisputable presence of another point of impact.

Florence, meanwhile, sprawled over half of me, crushing the whole left side of my body, and I had to roll over slightly to free myself, not that this put her in any sort of peril because, basically, she had already fallen and her fall now merely continued from a very small height, the equivalent—in fact—of my girth. I learned later that she was not even hurt. As for me, I was not sure exactly how I felt—a state I was beginning to get used to, mind you, especially as I did not know just how high my temperature had gotten during the evening, or how much alcohol I had had, or how disillusioned I had become . . . But, anyway, I think I can state that things were not too good. And, still lying down, I thought of the courage it had taken to get up earlier, and I relegated the prospect of another erectile effort to the limbo of an ill-defined future, not necessarily a near future either, I told myself. In the meantime I tried to move onto my side in order to facilitate, in the first instance, a sitting position, whatever form it might take, mind you. I would have settled for an approximation of the lotus position, but that was probably asking too much. At first all I achieved was a sort of Roman-style pose with one elbow on the floor and my chin resting on my palm, not quite able to lift my eyes (which bit of me could I lift?) to see that virtually all the guests had started to form a circle around me while Gilles leaned over me from one side and Florence from the other, the former asking if I was all right and the latter begging me to say I was. And, abandoned by any vestige of dignity, I accepted that all this concern should converge on me, and

I refused no one's help now, entrusting my elbow to Hélène who was struggling to heave me up, but also my armpit to Jean-Marc Neufincq's solid grip, while Florence—her again—put her hand on the small of my back, and all this pushing and pulling conjugated not to bring me to some triumphant position to mark the end of the party but, more modestly, simply to stand me up, which is what happened, although at the expense of my leaning my left hand on Florence's right shoulder, offered now to minimize the pain in my left leg which I wanted to avoid putting my full weight on.

So there we were then, she and I, in a sense ready to leave once more, save the fact that we would probably have to say good-bye again after announcing how we were—it was the least we could do—to the gathering that still stood facing us in a semicircle. As for getting out through the door with Florence without attracting too much attention, as I had planned, that was now no longer an option. But, in one sense, that was no bad thing, because the guests as well as our hosts would now think we had no ulterior motives but simply the natural complicity conferred by undergoing an ordeal together, giving our over-hasty connivance a foundation, a precedence as if by falling together we had inherited a past, so that—at the last minute—the relationship between us was rooted in indisputable common ground.

"Are you all right?" Jean-Marc Neufincq asked me, clearly expressing what everyone was thinking. "Nothing broken?"

"I took quite a knock," I said. "I'll have a bit of a bruise, it's nothing. You're all very kind. We're off now. Thanks again."

I said "we" without thinking, of course, if I had thought about it I would have just said "I" or rather I would not have said anything, so, oddly, it was Florence who had made me speak. Thanks a lot, I thought, now I'd like it if she took over because I can't hold out like this for long, leaning on her shoulder, and on top of that weighed down by the image of this impromptu couple we seem to have formed, even if that is not really a problem anymore.

"It was a lovely party, really," she announced, to my relief. "Don't see us out. Thanks everyone. Happy birthday, Gilles, good-bye, good-bye," she added, waving her free hand while the other held me by the waist as she wheeled me around toward the door. And this time I walked forward with her and did not turn back: we had done it, we had said good-bye, all I had to do was walk. Which was no mean feat, I can tell you, but I made progress and picked up my bag as we passed it. To think they're all behind us watching us leaving, I thought. Except Gilles who did see us to the door in the end, and opened it for us.

"Good-bye, Florence," he said. "Good-bye, Serge."

It felt strange leaving him like that. It was a bit abrupt, I felt. But I had no choice. There was nothing to stop me, later, from thinking about him with regret.

I thought about him right away, in fact, or as much as the pain would allow. As soon as I was squeezed into Florence's car, which was very small, having managed to get my left leg in only by sitting facing the sidewalk with both legs outside and lifting my thigh by cradling both my hands underneath it, then my right leg . . . anyway, as soon as my limbs were back together—but my thoughts were still scattered, well, everything in its own time, I told myself—I had one, a thought, about the Traverses, one that settled in, though it was not yet quite under control, still untamed so to speak, cut off from all the others and I made no attempt to master it, but in it I could clearly make out the dimension of regret that I had intended for later. But it was there now, that thought, precociously so, flouting the fact that Florence was next to me, starting her car, a thought for the Traverses well and truly there, as if I had left them a long time ago and their faces and kindness were suddenly coming back to me, wiping away any memory of annoyance. And that thought was almost painful, guilty, because in it the Traverses appeared to be victims of my prevarications and my mood swings, then of my casual attitude, abandoned in the awkward closing stages of that party, mistreated and then piqued by my passing presence. Still, I didn't do anything wrong, I told myself, I went to pick up their cake, I gave them a present, I said good-bye and thank you, perhaps it's just that everything happened too quickly, my departure obliterating my arrival with the perspective of hindsight so that the Traverses never truly had time to achieve existence, already relegated back to the oblivion of before our meeting, provoking an enduring and uncomfortable impression that the only thing left of their brief apparition, the only evanescent thing, was their erosion.

And that was in spite of the cake, I told myself. The portrait of Gilles on the cake. Which I felt had testified to the fact that . . .

And we ate it, that cake.

"We're at least going to have to stop at a pharmacy tomorrow," said Florence. "For your leg."

"And at a cell phone shop," I said, no longer thinking of the Traverses at all. "I need to buy myself a phone."

That was in fact a decision I had just made. I told her as much.

"Maybe," she said. "But some aspirin, too. At least some aspirin. Do you have any preferences for the network?"

"The network," I repeated but I could just as easily have repeated the whole question. I had never been asked it before.

"A service provider," she said. "There are three different ones. Do you know them?"

"Yes," I remembered. "I don't have any preference. I just need a phone."

"I have one, if you want. On a good network, with good coverage."

"I need a number," I said. "My own number. I need to be called."

"You wanted to make a call yourself," Florence told me. "That's what you said."

"Yes," I conceded. "I'll make a call. When I've bought a phone. When I've got a number. I want to be contactable."

"I understand," said Florence.

I didn't need to be contactable up till now, I explained to myself. I only needed to be able to contact others. But things change.

"I'm not feeling too good," I added. "I think I'll just sit quietly for a bit."

"I don't mind," Florence reassured me. "But try not to go to sleep. I don't live far away. We'll be there quite soon."

"Oh," I said.

I remembered that we had not in fact set off for Braz yet. That was for tomorrow. Which was annoying. Mind you, when I came to think about it, I did not hate the idea of getting to bed soon.

On the way to Florence's house I do not know what we might have said to each other. I must actually have gone to sleep. Either way, she did not have to wake me. I heard the change in the engine note.

"Here we are," she said.

I was a bit stuck in my seat. I could see the road up ahead, lined with trees overexposed in the beam of the headlights. Florence got out of the car and walked around the back, disappearing into the darkness. Then a light appeared to my right. A lantern above a front porch, lighting up an area of garden. An orchard to be precise. With a path through the middle. Florence came back to switch off the headlights and pulled my door open toward her.

"I'll help you."

She was strong. A bit too strong for my liking, but this *was* all to my liking: without her I would have been going to bed much later. But, ridiculously enough, I was not without her. She was even a blessing. I leaned on her openly.

Over a period of about half an hour we had touched frequently, and there was a growing familiarity between us, one that owed less, I felt, to what we said than to our physical proximity. Mind you, the fact that we did not say very much to each other—our rather patchy conversation stripped of all small talk—was also a tenuous sign of an understanding. Perhaps we did not actually have anything to say to each other. Or just had nothing to say. To anyone. So then.

So then, she was holding me tightly and we stepped intimately into the room where she had just turned on the lights. A large living room with a kitchen area, and

furniture that looked warmer than the walls, but it could
have been the lighting.

"No stairs to go up," she told me. "The bedrooms
are on ground level."

She took me along a red corridor. Pushed open the
door to a blue room. White bed. I ended up lying on it,
on my back. She disappeared, came back.

"I had some left," she said.

She handed me a glass of water, two tablets.

She helped me sit up.

I drank.

She took the glass back.

"Do you want to sleep *on* the bed? Or in it?"

I tried to think.

"I'll manage," I said.

"No," she said. "I'm going to help you."

"No," I insisted.

"Don't make a fuss," she said.

She undid my shirt.

"That," I said, "I can do."

I pushed her hands aside gently. I took off my shirt.
And then something really stupid happened because I was
vaguely curious to see what she looked like, this woman

standing facing me—given how long we had known each other. Now, instead of scrutinizing her and telling myself she was strong, seriously strong, although she was slim, very slim, with a muscular face, long hands, big eyes, green eyes even, as I realized much later, well instead of noticing any of that, I was thinking of *my* body, stripped to the waist, my nakedness, and I felt embarrassed, especially as she was taking my socks off, at the time.

"Here's one thing at least," she was saying authoritatively, "I can help you with. Just if you could bend your leg," she added, and she started to bend my leg.

"No!" I cried, and she took off my shoes. I clearly had very few arguments against her.

"Now the pants," she said.

Well, I've come this far, I told myself. And I unbuttoned my pants. I pulled them down over my hips and slid them under my buttocks.

"Take everything off," she told me. "You can't sleep like that. I'll forgive the lack of pajamas, but at least sleep with nothing on, I don't know."

"Neither do I," I said.

It was only to win time but it did no good, especially as, I might as well admit it, I was beginning to want to be naked in front of this woman. Well, no, not in front of her. In front of any woman, in fact. I was beginning to want to be naked in front of any woman, yes. And I said "All right, if you don't look," but without waiting to see whether she was leaving. I was the one who closed my eyes, and I felt her fingers on my hips. I found the situation really very embarrassing. But that suited me fine. I was happy to be embarrassed. And then to get over that embarrassment. There was something about this sudden intimacy that was like a gap opening up, a gap I was toppling into . . . toward what, I do not really know. But that was what I needed, at the time, to feel as if something was happening, I think, to arrange for something to happen, while not really having anything to do with it, not making any decisions, it was out of the question that I should make even the smallest decision. So I was now naked, with my eyes closed, and with this woman's hands busying around my ankles, and the question of whether or not I should open my eyes presented itself to me, because, under the circumstances, keeping them closed would have taken on some meaning, it was bound to, and I did not want it to have any meaning, at the time my life would have suffered had it taken on any meaning.

Unless, I told myself, it's because I'm tired. Acknowledging it was just tiredness . . . that was keeping my eyes closed. Or even sleep itself. And that did not strike me as particularly stupid. So I kept my eyes closed. I did not go so far as to pretend to be asleep, it would have been pointless. Anyway, I did not have a hint of a semblance of an erection, from that point of view at least I was untroubled.

"You'll have to stand up a bit so that I can pull the sheets down," she told me.

Okay, okay, I told myself. Let's get up. Let's try and get up. I leaned on my elbows but it seemed impossible to proceed any further, my eyes open now. I could not exert myself that much without looking at things. Not at Florence, granted—she was now pulling the sheets down toward my feet, with the intention of then putting them over me—but, thank God, it was easy, at the ceiling, which was facing me. And I could feel the sheets coming away beneath me, creating another sort of opening, but nothing toppled, I was very soon covered over, as if, in short, I had been exposing myself and Florence was putting things right, acting alone to counter the immodesty of a man no longer in control of his faculties. I felt slightly upset by this then, when she said a quick goodnight and slipped away before I could react; I felt frustrated, I had an acute awareness of my body and, in the pit of my stomach, a warmth hotter than the fever and, to aggravate my tiredness, the knowledge that sleep would be impossible.

I considered, very soon after that but it was already late, that this woman had behaved badly toward me, far too natural and familiar, then too abrupt, that there was no reason why she should have left like that, basically leaving me alone to contemplate our intimacy. And so it was with a fierce, rancorous determination, with a sense of claiming what was rightfully mine (and I do not say that lightly, I had no intention of turning the situation around, I simply wanted to redress the balance), it was with fierce determination, then, that I struggled with the diverse obstacles in my way, the weight of my body that I had to lift, the alcohol, the fever, my leg that needed guiding toward the floor, then from a sitting position on the side of the bed, acceding to the next stage up. Funny actually, I thought to myself, how you can manage on your own in the end, sometimes. Because, with the help of pieces of furniture, I was in fact making progress, I was not in that much pain, or perhaps I was getting used to it, limping, using even the walls to support me. What I don't actually know is exactly where her room is, I told myself.

But I found her room. I would have crawled there if need be. I found it two doors further on, I did not yet know that it was her room, I clung to the second door handle I came to, turning it at the same time. The first had opened into a sort of office, or that is what I assumed in the dark, and when all was said and done there was nothing I could do naked in an office. The second was the right one. It was just as dark in the room, but I could hear slightly chaotic breathing, hers, no doubt about it, and I used it to guide me over to the bed, careful not to make the floorboards creak, not sure how—when I eventually reached the edge of the mattress—I was going to go about justifying my presence to the sleeping woman. I could not see myself shaking her. I would prefer it if she were warned in some way. It would be best, then, if she woke before I touched her, I told myself, and I soon thought of waking her, yes, but in a way that would not make her protest, and I knew exactly how to do it, but it was going to be tricky. Or, to be precise, difficult.

It was to fall over. To make a noise falling over.

There were two new obstacles hampering this plan: on the one hand, I had not yet recovered from my earlier fall, far from it; on the other, I did not know how to fall over. I still do not know. The ensuing fall taught me nothing on the subject. In fact, there was nothing voluntary about it. An armchair I was still leaning on before making up my mind to let go of it with a view to landing noisily on the floor, while preserving what little good health I had left, turned out to be on casters and I slipped backward, landing on my coccyx and experiencing such pain that I gave an involuntary cry.

I may as well say that I hardly felt fond of Florence at that particular moment. Lying naked on the floorboards in the bedroom of a woman who, judging by the evidence, has some reason to carry on sleeping—though not necessarily without me, I thought—and who does not even wake up to help me when nothing has been spared in raising the alarm . . . well, it's a pretty regrettable situation, and I'm going to have to get out of it. But how? I asked myself, because she still hasn't woken up and I'm in pain and I resent her for it, and I want to get into bed with her in spite of the pain, what am I saying, because of the pain: this woman who is still stubbornly sleeping probably has no idea that the damage I have just done to myself—far from holding me back—is actually spurring me on to demand compensation from her. And as my fumbling hand encountered the encouraging feel of the edge of the mattress, I pulled myself alongside it with my right forearm, soon relieved in its efforts by the left arm, and then I managed to heave myself up then to land, exhausted, on my stomach beside Florence who was still asleep, which I initially saw as a stroke of luck because, I told myself, if she had woken in the final stages of my endeavor, I might well have been lacking great rigor in the explanations she would have had every right to demand as to the meaning of my behavior.

In the meantime, I did not mull over a single syllable of justification in my head. I did not care, in fact. What I was interested in, while the shooting pains at the base of my spine diminished, was finding the place where the top sheet, which I imagined was folded over somewhere near me, would open up a route toward Florence for me. And, just as I had already found the bedroom, I now found the route. If I am to be rigorously honest, I should point out that the phases of my enterprise did not follow one another all that clearly. Before slipping under the sheet I had already come in contact with Florence, inadvertently, when I was still lying on top of it, the sheet, I mean. She did not react then, either.

I carried on along my route, which was quite short in fact, I was there right away, in Florence's arms, coming from this side. She was turned toward me. And, as my right hand came down onto her waist, which allowed me to ascertain that she slept naked (just as she encouraged her guests to sleep!), my face came close enough to hers to touch it. I knew it, I could feel her breath. I could even make out, as you can in the dark, the contrasting pallor of her skin, and I was afraid that, if she should wake right then, she might have a heart attack. In any event, I had no intention of putting my lips to hers, or to her cheek, I did not want to. I, therefore, needed to avoid any kind of confrontation, and I resolved, as she still showed no reaction, to gravitate toward her breasts. And that was when I realized it was too much, way too much. And that what I needed, then, in the most urgent way, was to sleep. Which I did, I seem to think, quite quickly, although I did have the sensation of cupping all or part of a breast—whose elasticity obsessed me—while Florence's hand closed over the nape of my neck.

The next morning I woke up beside a woman who was not mine, in a bed that was not ours in a room that had been decorated without my being consulted. Great, I started saying to myself, and the memories did actually come back to me gradually, I'm not at home, but Laure *is*, she is at home, without me, a long way from here, and here I am starting a new day without her, with this woman who means nothing to me next to me, and naked too, and—unfortunately—waking at the same time as me. What should I do? Say good morning to her?

Because our eyes met—or at least the rudiments of visual perception attempted from beneath our half-opened lids did. They met and then darted away, using a series of successive approximations to identify each other, even closing again, once they were sure of what they had seen, to open once more on the known world. During this process we emerged from sleep, reaching a clearer and clearer consciousness of our reciprocal unfamiliarity, embarrassed by our memories of the night, hesitating (at least I imagined Florence was) to pick up the thread of our physical proximity, as if that would have meant breaking the ice all over again, even going so far as to have the verbal exchange we had so openly done without a few hours earlier. As for me, I was not in the same state as the day before at all, the fever had dropped and the alcohol dissipated, only my leg was hurting but not my last vertebra. I seemed to be able to move. I wanted to move, in fact, to get up and to leave. Not without her, though. I remembered her offer of a lift. And it was that offer that stayed with me because, in the morning, Florence was reduced to that offer of a lift she had made the previous evening, from before my anger and before the extinction of that anger. And with the active participation of the daylight I now discovered her breasts, still loaded with the same power and fully armed by the light but held back by what little shadow was left in the room; and her eyes that were so green you could not fail to notice them, bright enough to be remembered and deep enough to get lost in if, that is, you were prepared to be . . . but I was not, if I was prepared for anything it was to leave, and I did not want to do anything to compromise that departure, and that is probably why I did actually say good morning to her.

She could not really hold it against me because I had said it softly, attentively. And the fact that my hand was not, at the time, touching her might have been misinterpreted, as could my slight recoiling when I was afraid she was moving closer to take me in her arms, attempting a sort of crawling movement, it seemed to me, but none of that altered the fact that I had said good morning to her and I was smiling at her, and that smile prohibited any intimate gesture from her, freezing her in a state of gratitude. She then smiled too, given that she was obliged to interpret my politeness as propriety, but also that—confronted with my apparent kindness—she was incapable of going beyond that propriety by taking the risk of demonstrating a desire she was not absolutely sure I reciprocated. She returned my "good morning" as if it were quite normal, as if I were simply shy, embarrassed to discover there were consequences to the exchange we had had the night before, and that—with nothing better on offer—we should make the most of the opportunity we were being given, by our plans to leave for Braz, to escape the difficult question of renewing our physical exchanges.

To be honest, it hardly matters by what route we finally managed to get up without touching each other that morning, we did get up and from that moment on, as we got ourselves ready, we sloughed off our intimacy so that—as the time to leave drew closer—the untidy sheets seemed to represent a dead skin, testimony to a previous phase that was now over. And I congratulated myself on this state of affairs especially, I told myself, as returning to the earlier phases by which we reached it was becoming optional and, in my case, out of the question. I don't know how *she* feels about this but, as far as I'm concerned, the whole thing is dealt with. At worst I'll just have to hold her back, telling her she should be careful because we're on the road, yes, that's it, and she'll be driving too—I remembered we had agreed to that the night before.

She was not completely ready, I was, in spite of the trouble I had had bending my leg while getting dressed. Quite a lot of trouble, but enough of that. So I watched her surreptitiously, and she was a stranger. And I was too. When all was said and done we were worlds apart, particularly me, I told myself, but not only from her, from everything, from myself, from the previous day. . . . That's it, I told myself. It's yesterday that's a world away. The party yesterday. The whole day. As for the day before, that's ancient history. I was almost still young then. Too long ago to remember. And, when you get to the age I am now, the present is all that matters: this woman, then, Florence, I am setting off with her and I absolutely have to get rid of her by this evening. In the meantime it's going to be a question of co-existing.

Of tolerating her, to start with. Of fostering the conversation a bit, no more. Stopping for lunch, a sandwich, and I can use that time to buy a phone. I will ask if she would like to help me. I will make her part of it. I will remain polite, sufficiently dependent on her for her to recognize what she is doing for me because, first and foremost, this woman helped me. She will continue to do so. I might even be a little sad during the journey. A little anxious. No more fever, but anxious. Nothing's ever right with you, she will be able to say. There's always something wrong. I will agree. That will make me bearable. She will have to tolerate me, too. Perfect, I told myself.

"Can I help you?" I asked her.

I offered to carry her bag to the car, it seemed the minimum I could do for her and the maximum I could manage. Florence walked ahead of me, key in hand, supple . . . she could very easily have appealed to me with her pencil skirt, her narrow feet, her perfect shoulders beneath the blouse that, earlier, I had watched her finish putting on after a few failed attempts, most of which she had done out of my sight, eventually walking past me without seeing me, the busy woman who does nothing to disguise the flash of white skin revealed as she passes a man.

"You seem to be feeling better this morning," she did almost snap at me, though, as if wrapping the words around herself instead of the side of her blouse that still hung free.

So there I was behind her, walking toward the car, limping terribly, yes, but she had not noticed that, secretly suffering, I suppose, each step bringing me not so much to the end of the distance I had to cover than, at each moment, to the point of crying out. But in spite of my pain, I had a fairly clear idea of what was to come next, my mind was free, in fact, and completely preoccupied with the thought of Laure whom I would soon get hold of by telephone, and this would mean she could do the same to me, even if, as usual, she had nothing to say to me. And I was reassured by the fact that she would now be able to call me, not that I was sure she would end up doing so. But she would have in her possession a number, and all she would have to do was dial that number to speak to me, which would make her not exactly the same person. Armed with this number, Laure would change in some way.

Because her silence, if it continued, would take on a new color. And I would not have staked my future on the fact that she could bring that color to life. I could already imagine her with my number, you see, it was bound to be written down somewhere, on a piece of paper or in a book, wherever, somewhere she would not have to look if she were not intending to use it. I imagined what this choice would imply in terms of avoidance and distance, attitudes that—while she had first adopted them two days previously at the hotel—would take the form of a confirmation that she would have to find the courage to express. And I think I found it reassuring, the fact that, in those circumstances, Laure would still have something to do. And that everything she did, from that point onward, would be something.

Even if, I did point out to myself, Laure already thought she was able to get hold of me by calling Philippe's house, where I was supposed to be. I had hardly thought about that until now, and I did think about it but I told myself there was little danger of Laure calling Philippe. I am there with him representing her, she made that pretty clear. And, in any event, she will never succeed in getting ahold of me like that, by going through Philippe. And anyway, I told myself, I don't care, let her call Philippe if she feels like it: she'll soon see I'm not there, it wouldn't do her any harm, or it would do her just the right amount of harm. Either way, she won't call, I know she won't. Because I'm the one who's going to call her. Quite soon, even.

There is also the fact, I told myself—as Florence opened the trunk of the car and I hurried to bundle in the bags, not sure I could hold out another ten seconds without groaning—there is also the fact that Philippe himself could call Laure. He has every right to be concerned about our absence. My only means of knowing whether he has done this, incidentally, is to call Laure. Which brings me back, in a way, to buying a phone. And in any event, as far as Philippe is concerned, I will arrive too late. His birthday is behind him now.

I still had time to notice, as I closed the trunk and the possibility of sitting down now drew closer (and that thought alone almost annihilated my pain), that I had never decided to warn Philippe of my delay, or Laure's absence. And, what is more, that I would not be taking her with me. It was the price I asked, this delay and the fact that no one was informed of it, that it should go hand in hand with my silence.

Galvanized as I was by the proximity of the passenger seat, now that we were just about to get into the car, I managed to sit down by clenching my teeth. And so I found Florence sitting beside me, starting the engine. She was distinctly pretty. That was not the question; besides, I was supposed to be parting company with her today and I saw that parting as a task. I had to prepare the ground a little, it seemed to me, to appear a bit frosty. And I was actually a bit frosty, a bit focused on my plan to buy a phone.

"You're not taking the freeway, are you?" I asked her, "because, you know, shops on the freeway . . ."

She threw me a glance that could have been taken as hostile, but perhaps it was too soon. Her glance suited me fine, anyway.

"But we're not exactly going to stop now," she told me. "We've only just set off."

"Well, a bit on the freeway," I suggested. "Then we'll come off."

"Once I'm on the freeway," Florence replied, "I'm never too eager to come off."

"There's the highway too," I said. "It does exist."

Our conversation easily tolerated being aerated with silences. I looked at the countryside for a while but did not really know what to do with it.

"Last night," Florence picked up again.

"Yes," I said. "We can talk about it. We can talk about that too."

"Actually, no," she said. "No. No point. We'll take the highway."

"Thanks," I said.

I looked at the countryside again. What I was really waiting for was for it to change. From the continental to the coastal, I mean. No signs of that sort of thing yet. Not much to see apart from the road, then, and Florence's profile, surreptitiously, the opening of her blouse under the same conditions, and this afforded me a permanent— and obscurely consoling—anchorage point. But, in the end, what I missed was words. The exchange of words.

"When we get to Le Plessis-Saint-Georges," I announced.

I had unfolded a road map, taken from the pocket in the door.

"For the shop," I said.

"I'll remember," she said.

I found myself just where I was used to being, waiting. Only in a bit more of a hurry than usual.

Obviously, I had my doubts about Le Plessis-Saint-Georges. The town of Vitré would have been more suitable, given that this was to buy a telephone, but in order to go there we would have had to veer a good thirty kilometers from the highway we had just joined. So I was expecting a great deal of Le Plessis-Saint-Georges, probably too much, and I suspected Florence knew more than I did about the little place, and in particular enough for her to be convinced that Le Plessis-Saint-Georges was not well equipped in cell phones. As for stopping in Rennes, which would have meant abandoning the bypass that sweeps around it in order to go right into the town, it would have taken too long, been too far.

I studied the map again, but, undeniably, before Rennes, if I excluded Vitré, Le Plessis-Saint-Georges was virtually the only place I could see that would do. Clearly, my plan to buy a phone without wasting too much time was ambitious. But, as I had no more modest plans at hand, I just had to give it necessarily serious consideration. And so I genuinely did pin all my hopes on Le Plessis-Saint-Georges, aware that this attitude had an element of disproportion to it, even that it demonstrated not so much hope as stubbornness. In fact, I was beginning to loathe Le Plessis-Saint-Georges, almost as if I had bad memories of the place already, and the idea of going back there was torture.

Still, we were on the road, and going quite quickly because Florence was a lively driver, perhaps she was in a hurry too, I told myself, which suited me whichever way you looked at it, and so we drew significantly closer to Le Plessis-Saint-Georges and the first reference to it— on a road sign—hit me like a punch in the face. The ensuing references after that, in spite of their smaller impact or even because of it, worked away at my body as if only needing one final blow, weakened as I already was by the rigors of a fight in which, what is more, I alone represented both protagonists, given that Le Plessis-Saint-Georges was of course only a fictitious adversary, at least so long as I did not know its true resources.

When time had passed—a little in geographical terms, a great deal in mental terms and then definitively in chronological terms thanks to the sudden resolution of its analogical components confirmed by the numbers on the clock on the dashboard—when time had passed, these road signs were replaced by a town sign that meant that Le Plessis-Saint-Georges was right there, a few revolutions of the wheels away, and we were even driving into it, although I knew that the waiting was still not over because I had to live in the hope that somewhere along the side of the road there was a cell phone shop, or it could just as easily have been in a back street, down by the church, for example, because we could see the steeple over to the right.

Le Plessis-Saint-Georges, it struck me, is quite a big place, an ugly gathering around the highway that rips through the middle of it, like those injured people you sometimes see curled over in pain, hugging themselves with their hands to hold together an open wound. And you know they will not make it. But Le Plessis-Saint-George was holding out, lining up its walls traced by exhaust fumes, punctuating them with doors and windows to give them an impression of life, occasionally—under the questionable protection of speed bumps—releasing inhabitants from one side of the road to the other, or even along the sidewalks, where their reflections were picked up in the windows of shops selling household electrical goods, food shops, hairdressing salons . . . and perhaps a cell phone shop, I told myself, but not two of them, anyway I was beginning to be able to confirm—as we drove through it—that Le Plessis-Saint-Georges would not accommodate two cell phone shops. One, then, was still possible.

"I'd rather you went a bit more slowly," I said to Florence. "We'll miss it at this rate."

"I'd be surprised if we found one," she told me.

"We could go toward the center of town," I said.

"We're in the center," she told me.

"The church is set back," I pointed out to her. "Over there on the right. We could go as far as the church."

"Let's get to the sign at the other end of town first," she suggested.

I was afraid, with this, that, having started the motion, Florence would take us right out of Le Plessis-Saint-Georges before I could make the most of all its possibilities. But she behaved honestly and did a U-turn as we came out of the agglomeration that was fraying off into industrial zones and where the ground was dotted here and there with road signs like ugly weeds, bearing improbable names for destinations where nobody lived.

When we turned toward the church, I encouraged Florence to go along the street slowly, then, after the church, equally slowly along those that followed. There were still shops on these streets, but fewer and fewer of them, and I told myself that—short of a miracle—no cell phone shop was going to spring up next to an old washhouse to put an end to this waiting and suddenly relieve my eyes worn out from looking and anticipating, relieving and surprising them with its shop window populated by little handsets available with or without a contract . . . now it was probably something to do with this rising technology that, in spite of its exiled status, Le Plessis-Saint-Georges *was* equipped with one, it did have one, a cell phone shop, there it was, next to an *auberge* with a gourmet menu—mind you, you would have to know it was there to go there, but then the people of Le Plessis-Saint-Georges knew it, *they* knew it was there, their cell phone shop, not far behind the church, there were even a few of them hurrying beneath its reassuring neon signs.

"You see," I said. "I was right."

We were there, then. Florence parked, a little way away because, oddly enough, there were very few spaces on this street, and we got out of the car. To be precise, I tried to get out while my driver, noticing the difficulties I was having, walked around the car to come and help me.

My left leg, in fact, having maintained a deceptively pain-free state due entirely to my immobility, now hurt terribly as soon as I envisaged moving it a millimeter, and I wondered what it would be like when I did manage to get to my feet, an objective that—in spite of help and encouragement from my companion whose repeated efforts petered out in the face of my inertia, like the backwash of a wave—now seemed a distant reality like some feat for which I had not prepared myself.

"Right," she said, letting go of my arm, "you don't need a phone so much as an anti-inflammatory and, first and foremost, a doctor. I'll ask in the shop where I can find one."

"Florence," I said.

She was just about to close the door.

"I don't want to see a doctor," I explained. "I don't want to waste time with a doctor. I'm very happy to take an anti-inflammatory, fine. Something pretty strong, but without a prescription. But what I really want is a phone. I'd like you to go into this shop and buy me a phone, Florence. I'll trust you on the choice of model. Wait. Here's my credit card."

So there I was alone behind the church in Le Plessis-Saint-Georges, worried about my leg, but also impatient for Florence to acquit herself of her mission, these two mental dispositions gradually allying to form a plan, which was soon very clear: to call Laure outside, some way away from the car, so that I could be in peace, while Florence waited in the car. I did not really want to make her wait outside. Besides, I wanted to test out my mobility, knowing that I would have to cope on my own at some point.

I pushed the door open. Easy. By leaning against the back of the seat I swiveled my right leg outside. Then, using both hands and clenching my teeth, my left leg. I was back to the position in which I started, from the Traverses' house the previous evening. All I had to do now was pull myself up. Alone.

The roof of the car, I told myself. On one side. On the other, the top of the door. Arms up.

Traction. I was lifting myself up on my own. Rather pleased with myself. No signs of a fever anymore, I noticed. Or a cold. A blocked nose, but that was all. The usual. And on my feet, now. With support, granted. My forearms resting on the roof of the car. Let go, just to see.

There were some people passing. Even behind the church people passed in Le Plessis-Saint-Georges. I waited a while. They went into the cell phone shop. I let go with one arm.

That was fine. It was more the other one I was worried about. I could not manage it. Obviously, I told myself, you just can't cope without something to lean on. At least. I hung on. Move a bit now, I told myself. See what it's like.

I took one step, then two, leaning on the roof of the car with my right hand. Then three. Come on, I said to myself. I went all the way down the right-hand side of the car. As I reached the back, I decided to work my way around it. My lower hand on the trunk. I was cheating a bit, my other hand was on the front of the car behind. To my left. I was making my way around Florence's car.

Obviously, I said to myself in the occasional brief moments when I felt discouraged, this can't really be called moving. Going around a car. And now I'm on the driver's side. Opposite my seat. But still standing. I'm going to have a break.

Florence found me leaning on the bonnet. With both hands. She had been much quicker than me.

"It wasn't too busy in the end then," I said.

She was holding a large bag in her hand. She ran the other hand under my armpit and stood me back up.

"I'm going to help you sit yourself down," she told me. "Until we find a doctor."

"No," I said. "A pharmacy."

"Get into the car, at least."

"No," I said. "I'm going to make my call outside. Would you mind getting the phone out of the box? And waiting in the car?"

"Don't stay there leaning on the bonnet, then," Florence said. "Sit down."

"I'd rather stay standing."

"Okay, I'll help you back around to your door."

She helped me again.

"You're limping terribly," she told me.

"I never said it didn't hurt."

"But you don't want to see a doctor."

"It's a trapped nerve," I explained. "Not a fracture or anything like that. I wouldn't even be able to move."

"Because now you can!" she said.

"I manage," I said.

We managed. I leaned on the roof on the passenger side while Florence opened the box. I thought fleetingly of the presents being unwrapped, at the Traverses' house. Then of Gilles's present. And, for the first time, of Philippe's present. Which I no longer had. Which was to be expected, in a way, because I was no longer going to his birthday. All the same. I no longer had a present for Philippe.

"Thank you," I said.

Florence went off to sit down at the wheel. I looked at the phone she had chosen for me, it was small and light, I had forgotten to ask her the price. She had given me back my card and the receipt, and I had put them straight into my wallet. I keyed in an access code, the same one we had chosen, Laure and I, for our phone. I called our number, still leaning on the roof of the car with my free hand.

Messaging service. I hung up, called our land line.

Messaging service. I left a message. Gave my cell number.

"You can call me back," I pointed out. "Call me back. Big kiss. Laure," I added, "call me back."

I called our cell phone number again. Messaging service, of course. I left a message. Not exactly the same. Almost the same.

"I hope you're okay," I added. "Big kiss. I'd really like you to call me."

I put the phone away in a pocket and opened the door.

"Wait," said Florence.

She got out of the car and walked around to help me. I sat down.

"Well?" she said.

I misunderstood her question. Or at least I thought I misunderstood it. Either way, I corrected myself:

"Pharmacist," I said.

She set off. Vaguely irritated. I could have done without that. I needed neutral exchanges. Frosty was becoming difficult with everything she was doing for me.

On the other hand, her irritation could help my cause. I could get annoyed, I told myself. After all. Instead of just leaving her like that this evening. She might mind a bit less, if I got annoyed.

It was easier, in Le Plessis-Saint-Georges, finding a pharmacist than a cell phone shop. Florence parked in a lay-by and opened her door. I put my hand on her arm to hold her back.

"I'm coming with you," I said.

"There's no point," she said.

"I want to buy a walking stick," I said.

She looked surprised. Then not.

"You do everything the wrong way around," she said. "You don't even know what's wrong with you."

"I haven't got much time," I said. "Could you help me get out? I need to try it, anyway."

She helped me again. She could hardly abandon me. It is what I would have done, I think. Except. A woman in my state, I told myself. I don't know.

There was someone in front of us at the pharmacy.

A woman. And there were chairs. I let go of Florence's shoulder to sit down. She waited behind the woman, well into her sixties, a great pile of boxes on the counter. The pharmacist, who had a nice face and a bright eye, was sticking labels onto them.

"It's for the man sitting over there," Florence announced, turning toward me, when it was her turn.

I hesitated to stand up. I nodded toward the pharmacist. Stayed sitting, in the end.

"What's the matter?" he asked me.

"A trapped nerve in my leg," I said.

"Have you seen a doctor?"

"No. I'll see one later. I know," I said. "I know. I just don't have time, right now. I'd like to buy a walking stick. In the meantime. Can I buy a walking stick from you?"

"I can always sell you one," announced the pharmacist. "There's nothing to stop me from selling you one, of course there isn't."

"And what sort of walking sticks do you have?" I asked.

"Crutches," the pharmacist expanded, "or T-shaped."

"Can I see?"

"Wait a moment."

He was extremely well put together, this pharmacist. He disappeared and came back with a crutch and a walking stick, both in plastic, one in each hand, and he brandished them instructively as he came over toward me.

"Crutch," he explained, nodding in the direction of the crutch. "T-shaped walking stick. The advantage with the crutch is that it grips your arm. It's more expensive."

"I don't want a crutch," I said. "Can I try the other one?"

Florence watched the scene rather absently, slightly embarrassed.

The pharmacist held out his hand to me. I took hold of his wrist and used the rest of his arm like a perch. I pulled myself up to his shoulder. It's a long way up, I thought to myself.

I took hold of the walking stick and leaned it on the floor. I had never felt anything like it. That sort of comfort.

"This is good," I said. "This is very good."

"Your arm is too bent," he told me. "May I?"

He held out his hand to take the walking stick back.

"Wait," I said.

I went back down toward the chair without letting go of the walking stick, sat down and held the stick out to him.

"We're about the same height," he announced.

And he set off with the stick walking around his shop, which was huge on this side of the counter, and I suspected he simply wanted to stretch his legs, or to see his shop with a new eye, this might be the first time, for him, I told myself.

"You see," he said, coming back over to me, "we both have our arms too bent. I'll cut it down a little for you."

Florence glanced at me. And I replied with a glance at her that meant basically there was nothing I could do about it, if he was going to cut the thing down for me, and I turned my attention back to the pharmacist, and Florence did too, in fact, because he was reappearing from the back of the shop gripping a little wood saw. Then he drew a stool over and rested the walking stick on it with one hand, having carefully taken off the rubberized end, and with the other hand—good and strong as he was— he started sawing with a steady regular action that he seemed to be used to, either because he was in the habit of sawing down walking sticks or because he liked to do manual jobs at home, it hardly mattered, there was a brief woodworking moment during which the piece he wanted to saw off resisted, then fell, restoring silence in the shop where there were now quite a few people. Spectators, really.

"Fabienne!" called the pharmacist, coming out into the customer area to present me with the walking stick while Fabienne, a small woman with dark hair and glasses, emerged from the depths of the shop, blinking slightly in the neon lights, and dealt with a tall blond woman deploying a hankie and speaking in a nasal voice.

"Try it and see," the pharmacist told me, and he helped me get up. I steadied myself with the help of the walking stick.

"That looks better," he told me.

"Very, very good," I said.

"Really good?" the pharmacist asked, concerned.

"I think so," I said.

"Because otherwise I could cut off another little bit," he told me, "but I'm afraid it might be too short then, and I wouldn't be able to make it longer again," he added with half a smile. "That's always the problem with these walking sticks, they're obviously not telescopic so you always have to make up your mind at some point."

"But I really think this is right," I said, and I looked at the pharmacist who was looking at the walking stick with a strange expression, it seemed to me, I wondered whether—deep down—he actually wanted to saw off a bit more for me, from this stick, because he was a perfectionist, or because he had an urge to saw, all of a sudden, and I had to tell him again: "No, it's perfect."

But he added, "Walk about for a bit, anyway, here, so that we can get an idea, it would be wiser."

Even though I was now embarrassed by the other people who were pretending not to be interested in me, I set off on a little circuit, for what it was worth, as a sort of test but, all in all, yes, I did feel quite mobile, less doleful, experiencing something close to delight at coordinating my footsteps in this new configuration in which I had to take into account a third element, while still maintaining —and herein lay the problem—a binary alternation. But I managed it. Mind you, I would have preferred to test it out properly outside, and for a moment I hesitated, thinking I might ask the pharmacist whether I could practice a little on the sidewalk, before making up my mind, well, after all, this was not a pair of shoes, there was no real danger I would dirty it, his walking stick, but, in the end, no, I did not dare, besides, don't exaggerate, I told myself, it won't make much difference. And—having decided I would take the thing, the walking stick—I finished my circuit, watched by the pharmacist and Florence but also by the blonde who was setting off with her medication, pausing opposite me as if to blow her nose, she did blow her nose actually but that was not enough of a pretext, even Florence glanced at her, and I stood there leaning on the knob of my walking stick and looked at them both, one of them familiar at the moment (Florence, I mean), the other—going by the evidence—only seen in passing, and she did pass me, in fact, and left. Florence and I were left there facing the pharmacist, and I asked him for an anti-inflammatory as well as the stick.

"I'll give you this," he told me, coming back with a box, "since you don't have a prescription. It'll be just what you need. Take two every four hours, and then go and see a doctor, okay? Don't drag yourself around like that for three days, there are limits."

I thanked him for being so understanding. I was happy, as we left, not to be leaning on Florence's shoulder. Of course, sitting down in the car was no easier than before, and Florence had to help me again. Then she set off. I could tell that there was no longer a suggestion of anything much going on between us on the sexual front, and that was a considerable relief to me. Florence did not seem bothered by this. Now that she had me parked next to her once again, settled in my seat, with my walking stick on the rear seat, she was calm for a moment and she knew she was free to drive on. She even decided to get onto the freeway. I no longer had any reason to object to that.

It was one thirty and we had another two hundred kilometers to go. Things were shaping up. We passed Rennes without my really realizing at first. Then I noticed that we had been driving through Brittany for a while, and Brittany inevitably evokes its own coastline (although, of course, this is a false impression at first), so I started looking out for some sign that would indicate its proximity, but there was nothing, it was still too soon. I was growing impatient. I was happy to be growing impatient. A bit tense too. Florence frightened me. Too helpful. Too efficient. And now. I wondered how I would have managed without her. With my leg. She could not stop helping me, driving me around and inscribing herself onto the here and now that served as my life.

I could never love a woman like that, I told myself. Or perhaps I could, but quickly. That's kind of what happened in fact. Not love, no. Not at all. It will be easy leaving her. Especially as I've become pitiful in her eyes, with my leg. And my phone. Just some guy who can't stop buying new equipment all of a sudden. Outfitting himself. Who is less and less adequate just as he is. She won't even look at me. Just the road, directly in front of her. Directly in front of us. Let's keep going.

"Aren't you a bit hungry?" I asked her.

Some guy who needs feeding on top of everything else.

"I'm okay," she said.

"Maybe we could stop for a sandwich."

Annoyance, again. Or weariness. Or resignation. She was not protesting. Turned off two hundred meters further on into a service station that a sign had just alerted me to. Maybe it will happen all of a sudden, I told myself. She's going to dump me by the side of the road with my phone and a bottle of water. But no. I do not think she was allowing herself that option. A refusal to abandon me. Incredible how easy this is, I thought.

Too easy. I was beginning to feel guilty. Several times since leaving the hotel I was aware of mastering a situation without having much of a hand in it, and I had that feeling again, an impression of power, all the more marked because I was not physically capable of anything and I simply had to leave things to other people for them to see the situation from my point of view. Still, it was a bit much. In a way, I was lucky that Laure was not at all under my thumb. It set the balance straight again. So half the time I found myself tending toward waiting for her call, repeatedly glancing at the telephone in the hopes of bringing an end to all this . . . this journey, this birthday that no longer was one, this woman, my leg, who knows? But the rest of the time I felt a ridiculous omnipotence, it was taking hold, and I no longer knew what to do with myself.

At the café in the service station I decided on a sandwich of ham and butter on limp bread. She was hesitating, though.

"Take the same thing for me," she said eventually, "I don't feel like choosing."

I went to pay, she went back to the wheel of her car, we drove on. As I bit into my sandwich, with hers still waiting in the service station bag, I started—for what it was worth—properly preparing the ground so that our forthcoming separation was definitively marked out in the continuation of our lives. At first I mentioned how very busy I was over the next few days, then I touched on my love life, an exclusively telephonic one for the moment, and even silently telephonic, I pointed out, and I realized that by talking to her about myself like that I was distancing myself from her even more, as if my words could sum up our brief encounter in one fell swoop, right to the end of it. She did not appear moved by this, quite the contrary. Although she had nothing similar to talk to me about, because—judging by her silences—there was no love in her life to guide her, and I did not seem to be the right man, not at all the right man, to correct the situation.

"And, anyway, I'm not waiting for anything or anyone," she told me, "the only thing in you that holds me, the only thing with you that holds me, well, the only thing in me with you that holds me," she clarified, "that gets me hooked, I mean, that makes me feel good, if you like, is your selfishness, and I can't get involved with your selfishness, I don't really have the time. I'm sorry."

"Please, don't be," I said. "But it's not true. I'm not selfish. Even if, in a pinch, I am, I don't like it and I don't try to be, I'm not interested in that sort of thing at all."

"I'm not interested in it either, myself, but I do like it," she said. "I like you."

"Me too," I said.

"I just find you a bit irritating," she said.

"There you are," I said. "That's exactly right. We irritate each other a bit, you and me. We haven't got much longer now, anyway."

We picked up speed again. Without actually becoming coastal, the countryside changed noticeably. Particularly the road signs. Before the countryside itself. We were driving through the Morbihan region. With the gulf to our left, now, although we could not see it. The sky acted as a reference for me. There was suddenly a lot of sky. And those roads that we cut across at right angles, tiny minor roads leading off toward the sea, crossing ours that spread out wide. We were getting closer. More kilometers, more time, more silence. Quite a lot of silence. We were comfortable, the two of us. It was over. And we were driving, with nothing much to say to each other. Time, then. Naked time, or nearly. I was seriously beginning to think about Philippe. And about Laure, of course. It was the same thing. She'll call me when I get there, I told myself. My phone will ring right in front of Philippe.

I won't have a present. Just Laure on the phone, and him, long after his party is over. Surprised. I'll hand him the phone to speak to Laure, in fact. It would be like having all three of us there for a minute. Like it was meant to be.

From time to time I glanced surreptitiously at Florence. The end of our little . . . encounter. Finished and done with. Everything had happened just as I had decided it would, and in the best possible circumstances, except for my leg. But, perhaps because something was reaching its conclusion and because I had gone some way along the route Laure had mapped out for me (coping with various different obstacles in my path without really getting lost), perhaps because of that I felt a certain anxiety that began, in some obscure way, to lay siege to my reassurance. Sometimes it took the form of Philippe's face, sometimes Florence's, and sometimes also Laure's, Laure who still had not called. I looked at my phone regularly. I also watched Florence, troubled to see her so untroubled, as if—in spite of everything—I had treated her in an offhand way and this had had some effect on her. And I thought more and more about Philippe, about the fact that I was going to him without a present, with no intention of giving him one, with this delay that now no longer was one, and with nothing to say to him except, here I am, I came. It almost made me feel like leaving again, already.

Except that I had decided that Laure would only manifest herself on that condition, that I should go to Philippe, when the moment of arriving on the island was already over, finished, erased. I am working toward erasing things, I told myself. And in the first instance, and I am nearly there now, this road will be erased, then Florence. And I looked at the one and then the other, alternately, Florence willingly erasing herself as she drove along, peaceful, neutral, prepared to disappear. After the Traverses, then, and after the hotel, everything was gradually being erased in what I saw as a wake, my wake, while in front of us, as we reached Auray and as Quiberon was indicated on the signs, the countryside seemed to be hollowing itself out, emptying itself, erasing itself like everything else, and I could feel it, this erasing process, preceding me too, and that made me feel almost drunk, I noticed, not the same drunkenness as the day before, but as if there was nothing left in front of me either, nothing that would put up any resistance to my steady progress and I was floating now, freed from everything. Not just

freed, I thought (or rather I felt, because I was not thinking, was not trying to think) not just freed but free. And
I touched my phone in my pocket, and that contact was
like a thought, right there, yes, now, it was a thought, I
thought that Laure no longer was, *she* was no longer free,
in fact, because I was keeping her shut away, that it was
my freedom I had acquired by buying a phone, my freedom to reduce her, Laure, to this phone, because all that
I now expected of her was her call.

Laure, I then knew, although I still did not quite
know what to do with the fact (meanwhile we finally left
the main road and set off on the D768 while the countryside opened out, still hollowing itself out, invaded by the
sky), Laure had reduced herself to the sound of her voice,
to an anticipated sound, and even before that sound to
the ring-tone that would precede it, and in fact I had no
idea what sort of tone that ring would have because the
machine had never rung, in the same way as I had no idea
what sort of tone the call would have; in fact, so convinced
was I that Laure would call when I was with Philippe that
I began to feel a new curiosity for my phone, as if it were
some mysterious object and I had to wait until I used it
for its true purpose to be revealed. And I started to feel a

practical side of me developing, something I had never really been blessed with before, a practical side that was becoming sharper in fact and that—as our route became clearer, there was no turning back, we had passed the turning to Carnac—led me to ask Florence when and how she was reckoning we would embark for the island, whether she had made any inquiries.

"Because I haven't," I said. "I'm not the one who."

"I'm stopping at Quiberon," she replied. "I need to see someone before Braz. You could just take a taxi-boat, I'll drop you at the quay."

At the time we were driving along the Penthièvre Isthmus, and the sea was there, on either side, just as Florence was talking to me about a boat and as that word resonated through me, rhyming with the word float as we—you could say—carved through the water, because the isthmus is only short. We were driving through land again, already, we came into Saint-Pierre and we had to slow back down. I did not know what else to say: so Florence was leaving me then, and this seemed very abrupt to me, I had imagined something progressive. Florence disappearing, yes, but not so quickly, not quite so quickly. I felt absolutely no regrets, incidentally. I had just gotten used to her. More particularly, I was surprised that she was preempting me in this separation that, logical though it was, had taken the form of a project for me.

Still, I was not short of projects, waiting for this phone to ring, for Philippe to appear at last, and, until you get to the quay I told myself, to make the most of your position, of the sitting position you are in, for now, on this passenger seat where this woman has had the generosity to put you, as well as her bed, because later you're going to find you have to get up, with your leg, and she won't be there anymore, you'll only have your walking stick to keep you up. And, yes, I made the most of the situation, I made the most of it for a quarter of an hour. We were in fact in Quiberon now, the road sloped more steeply and suddenly, turning the corner past a women's clothing shop, there was the open sea, water all the way to the horizon, intercut by harbor buildings, car parks, quays, boats, and the sky.

Florence parked.

"There," she said. "I'll leave you here. I'll catch a boat later. After my visit."

From where we were I could see a quay dominated by a notice board referring to taxi-boat reservations, and, moored along the quay, was one of these boats, its engine turning over just like ours, or at least this one continued to turn over after Florence turned hers off.

"Right," I said.

"Wait," she said.

And she pushed open her door, walked around the car, opened my door, and held out her hand to me. I heaved myself up: I was still in just as much pain, still found it just as difficult to pull myself up, but once I was up and using the walking stick, having let go of her hand, I turned to face Florence.

"Well, good-bye then," I said. Right then, I told myself. I'll kiss her. To the side of her mouth, go on. And I did.

She did not shy away. But neither did she take hold of my neck, when I stepped back, to draw me closer and kiss me full on the mouth right here beside this quay where—judging by the evidence, for the few passersby who peopled this port outside of high season—we must have looked like some couple prey to a passion only exacerbated by their imminent separation . . . no, Florence simply reminded me that I had a bag in the trunk. She went to get it out and handed it to me. Then she got back into her car, gave me a wave, and left.

I watched her drive away, she did not look back, I waited for her to disappear around the corner and that was that, everything was quite clear, and all I could do now was head for the taxi-boat and try out my walking stick.

I had fifty meters to cover, more or less, and the first forty proved chaotic, compromised as they were by my inexperience at moving about on two different forms of support—one natural and one not—while the third, my left leg, only acted as a prop fleetingly, accidentally almost, when I leaned on it by mistake. All difficulties, I eventually realized, which stemmed from the fact that I had the walking stick on the wrong side, on the left, in other words on the weak side when in fact (although the pharmacist had failed to make this clear and I myself had not noticed during my brief trial in the narrow confines of the shop where, I now realized, I had cheated with the laws of balance) I should have been holding the stick on the same side as the good leg in order to relieve its effort at the point where the heel strikes off for each step but also on arrival when the right foot takes all the weight again while the left merely flits over the ground. And so, in those last ten meters, I had a genuine feeling of satisfaction as I moved without excessive pain, and when I reached the taxi-boat it became even easier: one of the three passengers already on board, a middle-aged man with a long forgotten tie undone around his neck, offered to help me down. The boat driver—who had glanced over to us, this man and myself, with a kindliness that he apparently granted us in equal shares—welcomed me on board and accompanied me and my guardian all the way to the seat at the stern where the two others were sitting, a man and a woman, also middle-aged only their faces were very downcast, they were wearing seafaring clothes and were holding hands as if setting off on a roller coaster. And it was next to these two that I sat down, the driver having, at that point, asked me to pay my fare.

The boat set off soon after that and it quickly picked up speed, in no time at all the port was behind us. And from my position at the stern I could feel, way over there at the other end, the prow rising high above the waves, and we the passengers, I noticed, soon had water up to our feet. It was coming in through a hole in the hull, a man-made hole—I checked—but, all the same, it seemed

as if the driver had entered into a race with this rising water, hoping to evacuate it by speed alone, scattering it in
our wake. Seeing the level rise I had to restrain myself from
looking for some suitable receptacle to bail it out but I
seemed to be the only one there who was worried and, in
the hopes that this would not be obvious, or would no
longer be obvious, I decided in desperation to make my way
to the prow alone with the underlying thought, I might as
well admit it, that being higher up, if we were going to sink,
I would be the last to go. But it was only an underlying
thought, of course, what I wanted most was to be somewhere quiet, and anyway I need to be alone, I had just finished with Florence and I wanted that ending to last a
while, to get a feel for where I was, right now, faced with
what was to come, how I was going to get through the time
that lay between me and my destination, the island that was
far ahead, invisible . . . because that's where I'm going, I
told myself, that's where I'll find out and now I know what
I'm feeling, I can feel that I'm not going to sink, obviously,
because it's on the island that that's going to happen, in
three quarters of an hour, on the island and not here, where
I've finished with Florence, congratulating myself for finishing with her, before I finish with this constant waiting,

and I looked at my phone but nothing, there was plenty of reception but nothing. That's logical, I told myself, perfectly logical, everything's fine, getting better and better even, let's get on with this, let's get on with it alone.

It was actually quite tricky moving about on board in those conditions, which went with the territory, a combination of rolling and pitching—the pitching incidentally dominating as the boat's prow dipped down at irregular intervals, smacking the water to an off-beat rhythm, either plunging into the deep trough of a wave or slapping too soon onto its crest, and these constraints would certainly have had their effect even on an agile individual who was steady on his legs but, to the fragile creature that I was then, armed with a walking stick that tended to slip on the wet surface of the bridge, they proved to be more than a mere preoccupation, making it impossible for me to let go for more than a split second from the fixed supports I felt I needed on the nonwalking-stick side in order to make any progress: the back of the seat at first, but also the rail, then the side of the cabin, and I had to let go of each of them in order to grab hold of the next before the prow plunged down again or one side of the boat rose higher than the other.

And yet I did manage to get halfway to my goal like that, now squeezed in the narrow passage between the cabin and the rail, on a level with the driver whom I could see through the window, sitting on the edge of his seat, having abandoned the helm because with one hand he was prodding a fork into a carton held in his other hand, steadily bringing up to his mouth what I identified as grains of couscous, while he watched the sea attentively. I found that reassuring but it did not stop me from continuing toward the prow, soon past the cabin so that I came out of my corridor, then stopping and holding myself entirely on the rail, with both hands, with the walking stick clamped under my arm, staring out at the infinite expanse of water to starboard before setting off again.

Some birds the like of which I had never seen before flitted past in the distance in very compact groups that merely changed shape, then they dived down toward the water, laying their black stain on it in the same aggregate movement, while the sea around them established the full extent of its size now that no land was visible whichever way you turned, because turn I did, still leaning on the rail I turned right around: it was the same in every direction, clear, limpid, permanent, with nothing to interrupt the view apart from the occasional boat so far away it seemed to be lost. I went back to my side-stepping progress, my hands chasing each other along the railing. I had spotted a bench up there in the triangle of the prow, and I was planning to sit on it. My walking stick, which was still pinned under my arm, was a nuisance but I did not want to part with it, although this was probably a mistake given that it had proved useless so far on the boat, but never mind, I told myself, I'm not going to start questioning everything again now, it's too late. And I reached the bench, but it had taken me some time, a long time, so that when I finally sat down the island was in sight. Basically, in the time it took the boat to make its crossing, I had gone the length of the boat, and it left me with an unpleasant feeling as if I had traveled and gone nowhere, and the whole journey was reduced to this impression of pointlessness. But the feeling passed and the island was now expanding before my eyes. Even if I had nothing to do with it, at least the island was getting closer, it was coming toward me in a way and more importantly—all metaphors aside—I was arriving, I was really getting there. And this kindled a sort of excitement I had never felt before, as I looked back, toward my life, perhaps it was the sea, the wind, the tiredness . . . I was excited, yes, soon I would know, and suddenly the note of the boat's engine changed, the sea became more distinct, slower, making each of its waves more precise, the jetty around the edge of the port was no longer silhouetted against the water, we were passing it now and the driver was maneuvering toward the quay.

When the boat was moored I let my fellow passengers get onto terra firma. I waved to the driver, stepped over the gap to the quay and landed on the cement, leaning heavily on my walking stick and contemplating the climb up to the village. Very few people here too, except for two men busying themselves with some lobster pots and my three traveling companions, far ahead, going up on foot, naturally, given that there were no cars on the island, I knew that, Laure knew that, she had been here before, but I had not, I had never set foot on an island and I was starting with this one. It doesn't look very big, I thought, but I knew that too, Laure had told me, what I did not know was that there was a hill, and quite a lot of blacktop, I reckoned, maybe it got better a bit further on, near where Philippe lived, although I did not have his address because, and I knew this too, there are no addresses here, the streets have no names, only the people have names, including Philippe of course: Fabre. Anyway, it was really close to the church, you just had to ask for Fabre, Mr. Fabre's house, when it's warm like this people are out on their front doorsteps in the street, you see, there aren't any gardens, no point, you can see the sea all around you and when you can't see it you can smell it, and all the houses are white.

I knew that, too. All the same, what I was really interested in was what I did not know, and I looked at my phone. There was a bit of reception. Enough for me to see that there had been no calls. Enough, also, for it to be able to ring should the situation arise. But the situation was not arising. One person in the world knew my number and was not dialing it. True, I had not yet reached Philippe, I was just starting up the hill. My first hill with a walking stick. And a bag, in the other hand. Difficult, of course. Manageable, though. I could go anywhere with that walking stick.

I met two people, going down obviously, and who seemed to feel sorry for me, either because they pitied my having to go up the hill in pain like that—because I never said I was not in pain—or because they generally felt that, with a walking stick, I should have been anywhere rather than on that island, I mean there are other places, after all, otherwise, in the circumstances, I would have to be there in order to do something crucial . . . well, I was there to do something crucial but I could not tell them, it was my secret, that was my secret, the fact that I had come here to wait, that I had come all this way to wait, but not for long, to wait and for it all to be resolved right away. So, guys, I'm sorry, I thought to myself, you'll never know, and I carried on up the hill without giving them another thought.

I reached the top of the slope—not quite the very top, there were still a good two hundred meters that carried on at a slight incline to the left—and felt the need to rest. I looked over to my right at a mini-market that was closed; in front of me at a car, just the one, with a caduceus emblem, parked outside a doctor's office; to my left at the incline that went on up to the village, where I could already see a hotel, some houses, and some gaps looking out to sea so that the street felt open, clear and white and swept by the wind. I found a bench to sit down on and recover my strength before setting off again, gradually making my way into the village, its houses sometimes huddled together, sometimes scattered to leave room for

flowers in between. A few inhabitants, too, or vacation-
ers. A couple appeared walking hand in hand, elderly,
dressed in seafaring clothes, I recognized them, they were
the couple from the boat.

"Ah," I said. "Hello again. Do you know the island?
I'm looking for Philippe Fabre's house."

They had both come to a stop, still with the same
downcast expression, and the man looked at me as if I were
asking the question at an inopportune moment, that I
should have asked it on the boat, earlier . . . well, that was
what I thought he was thinking because I felt he looked at
me rather severely, perhaps he resented me for leaving them
on their seat at the stern succumbing to the water while I
headed for the foredeck. It was actually the first time I had
spoken Philippe's name out loud, given his personal par-
ticulars, maybe I'm not supposed to do that, I thought, at
least not here, not now, that's it, this may not be the right
time to mention Philippe, I told myself, but I can't help it,
can I, I'm looking for him, for Philippe, I want to find him,
and in the end the man repeated his name:

"Fabre, Fabre, yes, I know him, it's the second to last
house before the church, isn't it?" he said to his wife, who
had not let go of his hand.

"I think it is," she replied, looking at me. "Yes, Fabre, you know," she added, turning to her husband, "it's the house where they repainted the shutters last week, the man who comes out of season, never shaves, and he always has that little red bag, a backpack."

"Yes," the man replied. "Fabre, of course. I think he's here at the moment. Are you a friend of his?"

"Obviously," I said, and the man looked at me severely again, with my walking stick, perhaps precisely because I was going to see Philippe Fabre, a friend of mine, yes, and so I set off: not only was I asking where I could find him but I was going there too, right away, limping, perhaps it was all too much for the man, such a show of determination, perhaps you were not supposed to go and see Philippe Fabre as a friend like that, right away, leaning on your walking stick, having asked where he lived, too obscene, I told myself, too clearly stated, thought out, undertaken, or perhaps they thought that I meant him some harm, Philippe I mean, that I was going to beat him with my walking stick . . . anyway, I did not ponder for long with this man who had just given me the information I needed, I was far beyond him in fact, he could think what he liked, I thought what I liked too. I could see it, the church tower, I only had another fifty meters to go.

So I was very soon there, in front of the second to last house before the church, it was attached to another house on each side, like most of them here, small and surrounded by flowers with a sort of little yard separated from the street by a low wall, the houses on either side had even more flowers but no patent signs of life except for an upturned boat in front of one and a cast iron pot full of geraniums in front of the other, complete with a plastic windmill that rotated intermittently in the wind making a soft clicking sound. And, in front of Philippe's house, with its shutters that were indeed brightly newly painted, there was a bicycle leaning against the window ledge. I walked past the wall, reached the door where there was a bell, rang it, heard its muffled ring from inside, waited a moment, I had a watch on, six o'clock it said.

I was still holding my bag in my hand. I waited, rang again, waited, waited some more, rang again, strained my ears, heard nothing. I put my bag down by my feet, rang again, waited, strained my ears again, checked that the door was locked, it was not. It was not even closed, just pushed to from the inside, the latch not connected. I picked up my bag and with the back of the hand holding the walking stick I pushed the door and went in. The shutters were closed on one side of the room, the sunny side, it was a real living room where everything happened, with a bar, a table, some chairs, and a sofa in one corner. As well as a sideboard with several things lined up on it, new-looking, as if they had not yet found a use here, in this room, not very useful things, actually, a vase with some flowers, too—presents, I thought. Presents but no guests anymore, I then thought. Or nothing. Everything was quiet, as if its time had already been.

I tried to announce my arrival by calling softly: "Philippe, Philippe," I said several times. I had not really had an opportunity to do this before, never in fact, except since setting foot on the island, I had not spoken Philippe's name because I did not actually know him very well, but if I had known him better there is no guarantee that I would have called anymore, so, seeing as I've come this far, I'll call him again, I told myself. So I said "Philippe" again and, as there was still no reply, I started to worry that he never would reply and I thought how incongruous my coming here was, too late and without a present, but I still called out again because this is what I had come for, to see him and it was vital that Philippe should be there now, and that he should let me know that he was, preferably pretty quickly. Either way I was not going to leave like that, I needed to see him, not so much wanted, needed, I was there and I called again as I walked further into the room, leaning on my walking stick, and he did not answer but I turned around and saw him, lying on his back on another sofa, to the right of the front door, his watch was lying on the floor next to a box of ear plugs and he had an open newspaper over his face.

So there he was then. Almost there. I still needed to make the connection. I had to let him know I was there, to wake him up in order to do so, to lift the newspaper. And, at the same time, check that it was him. I put my bag down. It must be him, I said to myself. I looked at him. I could not say anything until I had removed the newspaper. Open on the title page. A few hundred kilometers from us there was a war going on.

Before making a move I coughed. Not too insistently, mind you. My throat was a bit sore, my underlying cold was still there, all I had really done was limp over the top of it.

I was afraid I might frighten him. Then, even though my cough had had no effect, that I might suddenly disappoint him. When he woke up, I mean. With him seeing me there all of a sudden, empty-handed. Come for nothing. Not there enough, basically.

Let's lift up this newspaper at least, I said to myself. Let's get on with it. And I reached my hand toward the paper. It was exactly what I was supposed to do. Philippe was dead.

I am not sure what struck me most, at that point, the fact that he was dead then, eyes wide open and head tilted slightly toward me, or that my phone was not ringing. That it was not ringing because Philippe was dead. And the connection had not been made. Would not be made. That it was over.

That it was over between me and Laure.

Ever since the hotel.

Still. I would have preferred Philippe to live.

I calculated that, with my walking stick, it would take me ten minutes to get back to the doctor's office I had passed when I arrived on the island. I left my bag and went out of the house, having pulled the door to without completely closing it.

It was still warm outside with the same wind coming in from the sea, a feeble, hampered sort of wind, and

I noticed that one of Philippe's neighbors was coming out of his house, just after I myself had come out of Philippe's. He paid no attention to me.

As I set out toward the doctor's office I glanced back at him discreetly. He was standing outside his house as if taking the air, not properly dressed. Then he went back in. I carried on, hurrying on my way as best I could, attacking the ground firmly with my walking stick. I was in a bit of pain, over and above what was becoming normal. I must have been going too quickly. And it actually took me less than five minutes to reach my goal.

I pushed the door and came straight into the waiting room. There was only one person there, a man with a bandaged wrist, his cap lying on the chair next to him.

"Hello," I said. "I'm sorry but this is an emergency, I'm going to push in front of you."

I realized that he was looking at me as if I were the emergency. In his defense, I was grimacing, I was in a lot of pain again.

"No problem," he told me, "but perhaps you should sit down until the doctor's free."

"No," I said. "I can't wait."

And I headed for the door to the consulting room. Just then it opened. A man appeared, shaking a woman's hand, then he left. The woman saw me and gave me a questioning look.

"It's urgent," I told her, "I really have to see you."

"All right," she said, stepping aside. "Come in, what's the matter?"

And I walked in past her.

"Sit down," she said.

"No, I'd rather stay standing."

She walked around her desk and started to sit down, her face open, smiling, full lips, big eyes.

"So, what's the matter?" she asked again.

"There's someone who's just died," I said. "Well, I think."

"Where?" she asked not completely dropping her smile as if, it seemed to me, orchestrating a transition toward the serious expression that my words required.

"How?"

"In the second to last house before the church," I said. "Philippe Fabre. He's lying on a sofa, he's not moving, his eyes are open."

"What about you?" she said.

"Me?" I said. "I'm fine."

"No," she said. "You're not fine, I can see that." But she was already on her feet.

"I'm going there right away," she said. "Wait for me in the waiting room."

"No," I said. "I'm a friend, well, sort of. Anyway, I left my bag there, I'm coming with you."

"If you like," she said.

She pushed the door open and I followed her.

"I'm so sorry," she said to the bandaged man as she walked across the waiting room, "I have to go out, I won't be very long, I don't think, you could wait here or you could see the nurse about your dressing." And she left with me hurrying behind her, smacking my walking stick onto the ground in a quick succession of blows, and it felt as if I were suffering each of those blows. I must be coordinating this all wrong again, I told myself.

Luckily she was heading for her car. She opened the passenger door for me and sat down at the wheel. I sat down without too much trouble that time, that's odd, I thought to myself, perhaps it's getting better. She set off. We went up the street for a few seconds.

"It's here," I said.

She stopped, not really parking, there are no pavements there, opened the door for me, even helped me heave myself out and I followed her as she pushed the door of the house open.

When I went in I found her already crouching with one hand on Philippe's pulse, then on his forehead, sliding down. She stood back up.

"Does he have any family?" she asked me.

"I don't know," I said.

"It is him, is it?" she asked. "I don't know him."

"It's him," I said.

"Could you find me a blanket?" she asked. "No, don't move," she corrected herself. "I'll do it." She went upstairs. I heard doors being opened, I avoided looking at Philippe until she came back and spread the blanket she had found over him.

"I'm going back to the office," she said. "I'll call from there. I'll take you back."

"Okay," I said. "Wait, I'll get my bag."

"I'll take it," she said, and she picked up my bag. We went out of Philippe's house, got into the car one after the other and set off. Within a minute she had stopped, one after the other we got out of her car, she took my arm and we went into the waiting room together. The bandaged man was no longer there.

"Wait for me here," she told me, "I won't be very long, then I'll see to you."

She opened the door to her consulting room and shut herself in, and I waited, standing, leaning on my walking stick.

Not for very long, this time. She opened the door to me. I crossed the waiting room, stepped into her consulting room and positioned myself in front of her desk while she walked around it, sat down, and took out a form and a pen.

"Are you a temporary resident?" she asked, looking me in the eye with some underlying meaning, I told myself, I can see something there. Or maybe it was me.

"Are you not going to answer?" she asked.

"Sorry?" I said.

"It's your phone, I think," she said.

"Oh," I said. I could hear it now, there it was, the ring tone was feeble, probably not on the right setting.

"I'm sorry," I said. "I forgot to switch it off."

The ringing stopped.

I answered, "Yes, a temporary resident, of course. But I might stay, now. I think someone needs to stay."

"Yes, that's right," she said. "It would be better. In the meantime, I'm going to fill in this form." She looked up at me, there was a question in the way she looked at me. There was the way she looked at me, then, and the question, but mostly it was the way she looked at me.

"Yes?" I said.

"I'd like to know what your name is," she said.